Seven Hundred Seventy

Bogdan Boeru

Translated by: Anca Ciupa

Clink
Street

Published by Clink Street Publishing 2021

Copyright © 2021

First edition.

ISBNs:
978-1-913962-81-4 – paperback
978-1-913962-82-1 – ebook

Dedication

Chapter 1
Seven hundred seventy
(*Ab Urbe condita*)[1]

'Is there anything more vicious than the Scythian winter?'

The unspoken question paused the words about to roll off the tip of his tongue. Or perhaps he had just allowed himself a brief respite, to catch his breath after a dictation which had been dragging out for too long, when that thought, lurking somewhere, behind stifled silences, caught him with his mind guard down and pierced him like a poison arrow shot from the bow of who knows what barbarian from across the Danubius.

'Of course there is, but I do not want to know.' And, thus, he nipped in the bud something that could have turned into yet another one of his tearful elegies which he had never stopped penning and dispatching to Rome since the very first moment he set foot on the shore of Euxinus. He continued composing and sending verse epistles, even after he had lost all hope of ever being called back to his homeland. But now he refused to be consumed by memories, tears, sadness... He had embarked on a new project, *The Halieutica*.[2]

In truth, he was only deluding himself! He was doing everything in his power to take his mind off the fact that he had been banished from Rome and shipped... here of all

---

1 Since Rome founding date (Rome) (lat.)
2 *On Fishing-* unfinished work presumably begun shortly before Ovid's death.

places! He had learned long ago that there were far harsher things than the Scythian winter. He would have been ready to endure thousand times worse elements, if only he had been home. Home... A hollowed word... Yes! There are indeed harsher things! The difference is in how you look at them. As for him, the image of a centurion handing him the imperial order, at Messalinus Cotta's[3] villa, had been far more bone-chilling than the blizzards of the eight winters in Tomis put together. In other words, the eight winters in Tomis would have been unheard of, unless that particular centurion had entered his life right there, that moment...

He peeled his elbows off the table and leaned back on his chair to straighten his back with a painfully sweet stretch. He felt his spine cracking contentedly. The reddish light spread by the fire in the hearth was casting dancing shadows in the corners of the small *andron*[4] in his humble home. The room was warm. It created such intimacy you can only truly appreciate during a heavy winter, when you are inside and feel somehow protected in there, like in a cocoon. He felt like a message in a bottle aimlessly tossed about by icy waves, a heart obstinately beating in a dead body, akin to a sole surviving soldier still fighting the enemy, unaware that his legion had already been completely decimated. And that enemy was toying with him like a cat with a wounded mouse... A tragic soldier bearing an implacable destiny, yet, his current circumstances only made him feel laughable or at least inadequate.

From the other side of the wall, he could hear hoary Zia still pottering around in the kitchen despite the late hour. Seated opposite him, obedient and not daring to lift his eyes

---

3 Marcus Aurelius Cotta Maximus Messalinus (Ist century BC – Ist century A.D)), Roman senator, close friend and patron of Ovid.
4 A man's room (Greek).

from the wax tablet, dutifully holding the *stylus*[5] with his right hand while waiting for the dictation to continue, there was the young Damanais...

The candle in the candelabra to his left illuminated his beautiful, youthful features, which could not hide the promise of that clean and honest ruggedness all his kin developed with age. A teen Get, with hair cropped short in the imperial fashion, face to face with his master, a poet and knight of Rome, in a small room somewhere at the end of the world. So close, yet so far away! Both the two men and the end of the world...

The poet indulged in contemplating the tensed young man for a few more moments. He was no longer in the mood for dictating. The idea had fleeted... Besides, it was already late. He didn't have the heart to send the boy home in such horrible weather. He would order him to sleep in the guest room, not before stopping by the kitchen to ask Zia for some food, probably dinner leftovers, like salted fish, bread and a piece of *kykeon*[6] sweetened with honey.

Outside, the storm's dishevelled fury was raging through the streets of Tomis, wailing at crossroads and scraping with its icy claws against the hinges of front gates. The snow had already hardened, so the squall couldn't drift it anymore, which only seemed to infuriate the tempestuous hag even more making it cry out angry infernal howls that would have made Cerberus himself shiver in fear.

The poet was about to tell his much younger companion that their session had ended, when he heard something... Something different! Something different from the wind must have made that sound which had pierced the storm's incessant litany. It sounded like the croak of a raven, but not

---

5 Writing instrument (Latin).

6 According to the recipe, this drink could have the consistency of a semi-solid meal, specific to the Ancient Greek cuisine.

quite… It had been longer, deeper and hoarser … He shuddered at the thought that the Scythian night could breed monsters strong enough to face such a blizzard and make their presence known in a way that was so…

'Did you hear that?' he asked, pricking up his ears.

The young man finally dared to breathe, as if he had been waiting for a cue to relax. He understood the dictation had ended and he must have felt relieved that his master had stemmed his stream of words. He set the *stylus* carefully on the table and cracked his tired knuckles.

'No,' Damanais answered, casting an intrigued glance at the old man sitting across the table. 'What?'

He sounded confident as if there had obviously been nothing and the old man was hearing things conjured up either by his age or state of tiredness. He followed that with a brief shrug, leaning back on his chair and wrapping his thick wool vest tighter around himself despite the pleasant warmth in the room.

But Ovid frowned, trying so much to catch the next similar sound that he seemed to have metamorphosed into a human-size ear which continued its straining for a few good minutes without avail, however. He sighed. Exhausted, he ran his palm over his face, and then let his arm drop and dangle by the chair legs.

'Perhaps it was nothing after all,' the poet conceded softly… 'It seemed like a croak, but…slightly different…'

'Crows never come out in such weather' the boy replied.

'Yes… that's true…'

'You are tired, *erus*.[7] Should I tell Zia to get your bed ready?'

Ovid stood up with difficulty.

'Don't bother, my young friend. Most likely she has already done it. You should rather ask her to get yours ready,

---

7 Master (of the house) (Latin).

because you will be sleeping in the guest room tonight. If not even crows venture out in this weather, I can't see any reason you should.'

The lad smiled gratefully. He truly revered his master. More than four years ago (close to five), when he first became his apprentice and houseboy, he thought that the Roman was but an infatuated stuck-up. Rumours had it that, beyond all appearances and the exotic self-importance he was flaunting, the poet-knight, relegated all the way here at the end of the world, was only a whimper stringing artful words together to make the emperor relent and call him back to Italy. The meanest voices in town were spreading even more slander, insinuating that the poet, in order to forget about the emperor's constant and honest silence to his letters, used to drown his pathos (all of it) in some ephebe's behind...

Turning a deaf ear to all the calumnies delighting the slums of Tomis, Zourdanos, the boy's father, a ploughman who had worked hard to make a small fortune despite the poor hand he had been dealt at birth, slowly found his way to the great exiled and asked him to agree to tutor his first-born in return for the boy's faithful service.

Back then, Ovid had just lost Crispus, his old Roman servant, the only one to follow him to Tomis. He had been killed during one of the raids of the Gets from the left side of the Danubius. Ovid thought he was making a fair trade: the Gets had taken Crispus but they were offering him Damanais instead.

In time, the boy had understood that the Roman's uppishness was only a façade but not for a whimper or coward, even if the knight-poet was not really brimming with much of temerity either. Not that he needed it. He was a smart man, patient, educated, a darling of the muses. And the boy was going to become a good disciple himself. It had been quite easy for him to master the art of writing and reading. The poet's writing chest was full of papyrus cylinders smoothed with pumice stone, which seemed to hold the entire beauty, wisdom and strength ever put into words. This is where he had met Tibullus and his Delia, had joined the rhythm of Horace's hexameters and also discovered the greats of Antiquity – Antimachus of Colophon, Callimachus of Cyrene, the one and only Hesiod to whom poets owed their very craft, the illustrious Homer, Xenophon, Sophocles, Herodotus and many others. Thanks to their books, he learned about peoples he would have never heard of otherwise; visited wondrous places; rode alongside Alexander himself through the endless expanses of Asia, fought side by side with Leonidas at Thermopylae and came back to Hellas, along with the other ten thousand men.

He had found the immeasurable pleasure of reading and even writing, especially the dictation. It seemed the better his calligraphy became, the more he was morphing into the hand with which Ovid was writing his verses. And, to a certain extent, he was aware of the fact that he was partaking in creating works as grand and eternal as the ones in his master's writing chest.

As for numbers, he was driven to them simply by the need to get the hang of them, as he was in charge of shopping for the Roman. Even if the Roman was not in want of money, he was rather scrupulous about spending, without being stingy. It was just that he didn't want to fall prey to crooked merchants.

Right then, on that vicious winter night, after all that time by his side, watching Ovid trying to straighten himself and take staggering, old man's steps towards the warmth of the hearth, Damanais felt his chin tremble, close to tears. His was a sort of deep gratitude to a foreigner who, thanks to his instruction, had opened horizons never anticipated.

He was no longer solely a ploughman's son. He could proudly say, 'Behold me! I am the disciple of Publius Ovid Naso himself, one of the greatest poets in the world!' He felt chosen by fate.

The boy's little tremor and the flicker in his eyes had not escaped Ovid's notice. He replied with the same affection and an avuncular smile in his voice.

'Go ahead, child! Get some rest!'

And in the Getic language, to boot.

That moment they heard some knocks on the gate and looked at each other, puzzled. Who could it be? The Roman smoothed his long wool tunic and loose Get pants, which he would have surely spurned ten to fifteen years ago, as a Barbarian rag, unworthy of touching his imperial skin. He slung a Greek *himation*[8] over his shoulder, and sat back at the table, in a dignified posture, ready to welcome the nocturnal visitor, while the boy dutifully went to the gate to see whoever might be there.

Damanais returned quickly.

'It's a traveler, *erus*. He is probably lost. He is humbly asking for shelter.'

Without quitting his posture (that proud stance of a Roman, because a Roman stays a Roman even in the dirtiest latrine!), Ovid answered promptly, 'Evil times out there! Show him in! Tell Zia, if she is still up, to bring a piece of goat's cheese and some bread. If she is asleep, please do that yourself...'

'Of course.'

The boy was about to leave, but Ovid stopped him,

'Damanais!'

'Yes, *erus*?'

'It seems you are going to spend the night in the kitchen, by the stove...'

---

8 Type of clothing in Ancient Greece

'As you wish.'

He rushed outside, only to come back just as fast, accompanied by a stranger bundled up in fur, covered in snow from head to toe. The man shook off his coat and pulled the hood back on his nape. A rugged cheek, darkened by a short beard, steely eyes – no trace of fatigue, even though the outlander must have worked hard to push his way through the tempest, the frost and the darkness of winter to reach him. All these could have meant just one thing – the man was so accustomed to effort verging exhaustion, that he could only be a veteran, toughened in countless warfare campaigns. Either way, he was a warrior, no matter the colours he might have fought under. With a lump in his throat, the poet kept his proud posture and stayed as still as statue. He looked more like a senator wearing the *toga laticlave*,[9] rather than an exile banished from his own country. He did not know the foreigner, yet he had been waiting for him. It was as though the eight years of exile to Tomis had prepared him precisely for that very meeting...

He cleared his throat, mostly to control his tremor then made an ample inviting gesture,

'Welcome to my humble home! Please, take a seat!'

He pointed to Damanais's chair and the man sat down, dropping his heavy fur coat. The young Get picked it up. He was now holding it, awaiting orders. Judging by his clothes, the man did not look local or from some other place, either. He seemed to come from everywhere – a cap shoved on his pate, looking vaguely Phrygian (probably taken from someone with a much smaller head), a leather vest, with many belts and probably as many secret pockets, remotely resembling an armour, with a thick wool tunic underneath, with long sleeves and tightly wrapped around the body, like the mountain people, a Roman belt across his chest, with a

---

9 A mark specific to the Roman senators.

wooden scabbard with metal fittings, specific to the legions, which was supposed to sheathe a *gladius*,[10] but it was empty, a wide strap with Scythian adornments, and on his feet, on top of the loose trousers, he was wearing something looking like a cross between the leather, thick-sole *caligae*[11] and the Dacians' *opanci* shoes.

'Thank you, citizen Naso, for welcoming me to your house,' said the man, with a slight bow of his head.

Something in his voice and the fact that he had called him by his name ensured Ovid that the foreigner was the one he had been long waiting for. He had spoken to him in Latin. Judging by his accent, he could have been from the North of Peninsula, probably from Insubria.

Damanais flinched. Knowing what was about to happen and not wanting to put the young man in harm's way, the old poet tried to send his disciple away.

'My child, please fetch some food, as I told you.'

The boy wanted to go but stopped at the foreigner's seemingly soft gesture yet grave tone.

'The boy can stay here.'

His voice sounded categorical, yet worryingly calm. He did not seem to talk to anyone in particular, though it felt impossible not to obey him. Damanais froze mid-sentence.

'Foreigner,' Ovid spoke again, 'this concerns us only.'

After a few moments of thinking, the outlander nodded and the host used the opportunity to charge the young man as much as possible, just to keep him afar.

'Go, Damanais! See if Zia is sleeping! Don't forget about the fire in the guest room! Let it be warm!'

The young man left the room, not before he dropped the heavy fur coat by the door, while the foreigner was watching him from the side.

---

10   Roman sword.
11   Roman footwear.

With only the two of them in the room, the poet and the traveller maintained a tense silence for a few moments. One was trying hard to maintain the proud posture, of a true Roman, while the other one was scrutinizing his host, so as to find the breach in the guise of the old man sitting in front of him. It was only a mask, of that he was certain.

Finally, the poet broke the silence.

'I have been waiting for you.'

The other man seemed to relax a bit, as if those words had made his mission easier.

'Then, you know why I am here.'

'I confess I wished you had come here with a different mission. But I guess this is just as good…'

The foreigner nodded, then he looked around the room he had walked in as if he was seeing it for the first time, lingering on every detail – shelves, chests, two settees, the fire in the hearth, a cupboard… He stood up and took some seemingly careless steps by the table and the host's chair – but his 'nonchalance' took him straight to the chest with the scrolls – not the one by the hearth, holding the classics, but to the other one, smaller, by the bed, where the house master usually took his siesta. Fewer books were in there, but they were obviously new. The ones not yet sent to Rome.

Apparently absent-minded, the nocturnal visitor picked one randomly.

'The emperor…'

Ovid interrupted him, pretending to be surprised.

'Ah, the emperor… How is good Tiberius? Is he sending me his wishes for good heath? Long life?'

The other man smiled, not looking up from the papyrus scroll.

'Well…To believe that a man like ,the good' Tiberius, as you call him, might send you regards through someone like me, it means you are either crazy or careless.'

'Both are correct. Let's just say I have lost my mind while waiting for my recall home and, now, I have nothing to lose.'

The foreigner snorted ironically, pointing to the opened scroll.

'Aww! A treatise on fish?'

'Were you expecting something more… subversive?' asked Naso, putting on the most innocent look he was capable of.

'Rumour has it that you are working on something truly inflammatory. But look what it says here!'

Moving the scroll farther away from his eyes to read better, due to the small yet orderly handwriting of the young Get, the foreigner started reading and overdoing the accents, as if he were not in a humble room but on a podium, with hundreds of people in the audience,

'*Accepit mundus legem: dedit arma per omnes admonuitque sui: vitulus sic namque minatur, qui nondum gerit in tenera iam cornua fronte; sic dammae fugiunt, pugnant virtute leones et morsu canis et caudae sic scorpius ictu, concussisque levis pennis sic evolat ales.*[12] To me, it looks rather inflammatory.'

The poet shrugged his shoulders, in a gesture of apathy.

'If you think so…'

The guest frowned.

'The weapons of the creatures in the text are clear to me, but what is yours?'

'The word!'

'Hmmm… a double-edged sword'.

---

12 'The universe accepted the law, it gave weapons to all, and reminded each of their own. So come about the threats of the calf, who bears no horns as yet on his young forehead; thus do hinds flee, lions fight with courage, and dogs with their teeth, and the scorpion with the stroke of its tail, and so it is that with a light shaking of his pinions the bird flies away.' Ovid, *Halieutica*, 1-6.

'A powerful weapon,' concluded the poet.

The man put the scroll back, with an almost pious care then came closer to Ovid, who had stood up, waiting. As he had very well suspected, the guest's vest did have many secret pockets. With no hurry or any attempt to hide his intentions, the foreigner started undoing his many belts, on the side, without taking off his *lorica* altogether. From somewhere, from the bottom of the armour, he took out a Roman sword, wrapped in a cloth. Now he understood why the scabbard was empty, the *gladius* would have frozen in it on such weather. But what if someone had attacked him in the night? This is when he saw a Dacian *sica*[13] strapped on his back between the belt and tunic. A smaller weapon, the dagger fitted in a handier place, with no risk of freezing in an open scabbard. Why would he then really want to use the *gladius*? Probably as a statement...

Yes! It must have been a statement! Once he fathomed this idea, Ovid nodded his head thoughtfully, which didn't escape the other man's notice, the latter raising his eyes to Ovid for a second, to let him know without any words that he was right; then, he went on to unwrap the sword, put it on the table and did the many belts on his armour meticulously, not worrying at all that the old man might grab the weapon and use it against him. Each of them knew exactly the part they were playing in that scene, to bother with such unfounded concerns...

Once he was done, the traveller pointed to the sword on the table.

'This is my weapon.'

He picked it up and weighed it in his hand admiringly. He looked at the old man, as if he confessed that, unlike the word, the weapon was more faithful because it was silent. He came from behind, with the blade ready to stab him.

---

13 Curved Dacian dagger

'It will be quick,' he promised. 'I am experienced.'

'Wait! Naso stopped him. 'I want to look into your eyes when you do it.'

'Trust me,' said the man, with an almost friendly voice. 'You are not the first I am killing. Nobles do not usually want to see their executioner at work.'

'I am not a noble,' insisted the exiled. 'I am part of the equestrian order. More than that (with a bitter laugh) I have been stabbed in my back so many times, mostly by my false friends, that my skin has gotten so thick I am worried that your sword might spring back somehow and you might hurt yourself.'

The killer tapped him on the shoulder in admiration and moved in front of him, smiling in all sincerity.

'I was told you are a man of wise words and you truly are. Still, I was paid and sent here with a clear purpose, and you know that.'

They looked each other in the eye, as was Naso's last wish. Really close. And when the foreigner took out the bloodied blade from the old man's chest and supported his lifeless body, putting it back on the chair, he was able to read in the dead man's eyes something close to gratitude. He had neither been forgiven, nor asked to return home but at least his exile was over.

Nothing seemed to bother the traveller. Slowly, as if nothing extraordinary had happened, he wiped the blade on the dead poet's *himation*, wrapped it in the piece of cloth with the seriousness of the craftsman who treasures and preserves the tool that feeds him, hid it again in the vest secret compartments and, before putting his heavy fur coat back on, took those scrolls that Ovid had not yet sent to Rome. After that, he left, disappearing in the whirlwind outside.

Somewhere, in the night, a raven croak was heard, but deeper, longer and hoarser, over the storm's wail...

Chapter 2
Seven hundred seventy
– Damanais

He was damning the moment the foreigner knocked on their gate, cursing the winter, blaming himself for not having seen the danger hiding under that heap of snowed furs that was standing before him when he opened the gate. The man had simply terrified him. Not his face, fierce yet not threatening, or the unusual calm in his gestures and voice... Considering the dreadful frost outside, you would have expected him to be exhausted, in need of help, or to ask for a jug of mulled wine or complain about frostbites... None of this... As if he was not a human being, in flesh and bones, but a demon! There was something else there that had really scared... No, not even his suspicion that the foreigner might have come straight from Hell... But rather Naso's undisguised vehemence in sending him out of the room, as if he had already known something... He seemed to have been waiting for the man; even if he did not even know him, but he seemed to have been expecting a visit from the likes of him... One like...

'Oh, gods!'

It was only then, while fighting the blizzard on his way to the city's main strategist, Diokles, the son of Hippolytos, that reality hit Damanais so convincingly the boy instantly lost his balance and tumbled into the snow, not sure whether it had been the wind or the thought that had knocked him down.

He got back on his feet, swimming through the snow like a castaway in search of a board floating on stormy waters. He felt the skin on his cheeks cracking under the blows of the storm's frozen blades. It was the dead of the night, yet the streets of Tomis were lit as the moon and the snow blanket were casting light through the relentless ice fall. It was a light out of this world, from elsewhere, a place where no one wanted to be; a light that was sparking pain and fear, and spawning monsters in the corner of the eye.

He was damning himself for not having the wits to lie to the foreigner and decline his request to come in. He could have said the master was out. He was cursing himself for having pity, showing goodwill.

Right after he followed Ovid's behest and left the room, he knew that something bad would happen, but it was only in the cold of the night that he woke up from that mind slumber, that numbness felt by victims seconds before turning into food for their predators. He was blasting himself for not having been a real man!

His first thought was to run to Zia's room, even if it was not to hide beneath her skirt tails and shiver in fear like a coward.

'Mother Zia!' he whispered, gently knocking with the back of his index finger on her door.

With no answer, he tried again. A few slow and shuffled steps told him that the old lady was not sleeping. She had hardly finished cleaning in the kitchen for the day and gone to her room minutes before. She opened the door for him. The candle flame made her wrinkles look deeper than they were and turned her grey hair into a kind of nimbus. She looked like a spectre in her thick, white wool gown. Had he not heard her steps, he could have sworn she was floating, which would have probably made him run for his life, with his brain gooey and heart pierced by the needles of the worst fear. Otherwise, the old lady was a gentle, good-hearted person, quick to do her job around the house and with a smooth voice.

'What happened, my child?'

He had put his finger on his lips for silence and pushed her gently, back into the room.

'Mother Zia, there is a foreigner in the master's room...'

The old lady frowned.

'Who let him in?'

'I did, but that does not matter now. *Erus* seemed to have been waiting for this visit and I have a bad feeling about this.'

For her age, she was a quick thinker. She understood everything in the blink of an eye. Remembering her whispered commands now, while fighting the blizzard, he felt ashamed of the fog that had clouded his brain.

'My child, run to Diokles! Tell him to bring the guards! Hurry up!'

The old lady gestured for him to rush and then she locked herself in her room. Now, Damanais was battling the snow reaching up to his knees, draining his strength at every step plucked from its clutch.

In spite of the effort and the icy wind, the night was clearing up his mind; slowly, old images started coming back to him, bits of dialogues, barely caught glances, more or less random encounters – all these put together explained the scene he had just left in progress, in Naso's house. Yes! He had been waiting for a visit from that stranger! And, yes! The visit was a natural consequence of the past the poet had not left behind in Rome, but instead had taken it with him here, in the far-off Tomis, only to hide it in the verses sent back home – not meant for just anyone but for the ones holding the key to their meaning! And the key was alive, was living (or had lived) among them, they had been living it themselves and Ovid had put it in words.

A shard of life pushed through the snow banks towards him and lodged into his eyes. It had happened...maybe three years before, a little over... but not by much. He was carrying a basket with fish, just angled from the sea by the Histrian fishermen and had entered Dionisodor's house, the refined merchant and good friend of his mentor.

He had stopped for a few greedy gasps, as he had been lugging that heavy basket on his back from far away. He had put it down, by the door, before taking it to the kitchen. Ovid had been visiting Dionisodor for a few days, planning to stay longer, and he had accompanied him, as always, since he had been entrusted to the Roman by his father, the year before.

The autumn was young and mild. Things and people had a special glow, as if he was looking at the world through a golden pleura. In the inner court, the host and the poet were walking shoulder to shoulder, looking worried. Speaking in Latin. Dionisodor was a cultivated man. They had met in Tomis, in the archon's house, probably not long after Ovid had come to town. Old Zia recalled they had struck up a friendship so close that the Roman would not waste any excuse to take a trip to Histria to meet him. Sometimes, he would say that he preferred Histria over Tomis. It was a larger place, cleaner, more ... cultured. On his end, Dionisodor would not let too much time to pass between two trips to Tomis – even if his were for business rather than just pleasant visits to his friend.

The man was trading mainly grains but he also imported luxury goods. Later, after Crispus's death, the boy could testify as Naso's disciple and companion that things were as Zia had said – the two were seeking each other's company in true friendship fashion.

On that fall day, several words had stuck in his ears only so that they could now hit him full force... The knight-poet was holding a scroll that seemed to be an epistle from Rome.

'*Ante diera quattuordecim Kalendas Septembres*,'[14] said Ovid pensively, pointing at the papyrus scroll.

'Fate can be truly cruel, my friend, you should know that!' replied Dionisodor in his otherwise correct Latin, yet more high-pitched and somehow bouncy, where you could easily hear the Greek talk. 'Not that it had been too generous with you before. But, whatever .. It would be uncharacteristically hypocritical of you to say that you have never been in its graces...'

'True,' the guest admitted, nostalgically. You are right...'

The merchant stopped, making the other one stop walking, as well. They were now face to face.

'What I would like to say, my dear Naso, is that I am afraid... It is hard to even say it... I am afraid that Tiberius's taking the throne of the empire buries your chances of... you know...'

'I am aware of that.'

'And what you are showing me here, in this letter... For Dioscures's[15] sake! It is awful! It looks like a witch hunting!'

'It is a hunting. Agrippa Postumus,[16] killed by his own men, in Planasia?[17] Hard to believe...'

'Indeed! Please, don't tell me that you had set your hopes on him!'

'No, not at all! But his assassination proves to me how far Livia Drusilla[18] would go for her revenge. She was not satisfied with the convenient death of Octavian Augustus

---

14 Fourteen days before the Calends in September (Latin), i.e. 19 August (year 14), the death date of Emperor Octavian Augustus
15 Included among stars (Greek).
16 Agrippa Postumus (12 BC– AD 14), grandson of Octavian Augustus, banished from Rome by his grandfather in the year AD 9, probably due to warps coming from empress Livia Drusilla.
17 Island in Tyrhenian Sea, where Agrippa Postumus was exiled and killed.
18 Livia Drusilla (58 BC–AD 29), wife of emperor Octavian Augustus, mother of the future emperor Tiberius.

or the crowning of her son, Tiberius… She is going to kill everyone, down to the last one! All her enemies…'

Dionisodor put his hands on Ovid's shoulders and looked him straight into the eyes.

'If this is the case, I am afraid for you, too.'

The usual rosy tint in his cheeks, a sign of good fortune, paled away.

Not long after that visit, rumour had it that Agrippa Postumus was not actually dead but gathering an army to overthrow Tiberius. It turned out to be only a distasteful farce. The servant of the killed man, a certain Clemens,[19] who resembled his master so well that anyone could have sworn he was his twin, was exposed when he was trying to pose as Augustus's grandson. At least he got to confront the new emperor, before suffering his own death:

'How did you become Agrippa?' Tiberius asked.

'The same way you became the Caesar.'[20]

Not bad for the last words of a former slave, right?

Some other time, during a reading session in the *andron* of the house in Tomis, he had challenged his master.

'*Erus*, with all due respect, there is something here that does not seem to fit…'

Ovid burst into the most sincere and rambunctious laughter the boy had ever heard.

It was a rare opportunity to see him laugh. He was not an excessively sombre man and there was no question of him lacking flexibility as expected of an ever-glum tyrant. It was just that sadness had grown deep roots in his soul and left little room for the daemon of laughter.

---

19 Clemens (?–AD 16), impostor, former slave of Agrippa Postumus, who posed as his master after his demise, while taking advantage of their close resemblance..

20 Historic dialogue, according to testimony from Dio Cassius (*Roman History* 57:16)

This is why he let his master enjoy the moment while the peals of cheerfulness filled the room, as if the horn of plenty had spilt in there. It would have been inconceivable to interrupt him anyway.

Moments later, while wiping his tears, the poet answered to the challenge, hiccupping.

'My child, you... do you understand what... what you are reading... there? He! He! We are talking about... about...'

He burst out laughing again.

'You have there... Ha! Ha! Ha! They are... my *Metamorphoses*! Ha! Ha! Ha!'

But in the end...

'Please, excuse me, Damanais! Only a few criticized my *Metamorphoses*, and those are crowned heads! Or they were... I am dying with curiosity to find out what does not seem to fit.'

'Forgive me, *erus*! I did not mean to... But I do not understand... The iron of the iron age is hard, but we could not work our land without it, build tools, sail our ships... What is the connection to...

'"*Vivitur ex rapto; non hospes ab hospite tutus, non socer a genero, fratrum quoque gratia rara est; inminet exitio vir coniugis, illa mariti, lurida terribiles miscent aconita novercae, filius ante diem patrios inquirit in annos; victa iacet pietas, et virgo caede madentis ultima caelestum terras Astraea reliquit.*"[21]? I do not look at iron as an inferior material. Why would the justice goddess turn her back to the world, during a time described by a metal maybe not so precious as in the previous ages, but nevertheless useful?'

---

21 'They lived on plunder: friend was not safe with friend, relative with relative, kindness was rare between brothers. Husbands longed for the death of their wives, wives for the death of their husbands. Murderous stepmothers mixed deadly aconite, and sons inquired into their father's years before their time. Piety was dead, and virgin Astraea, last of all the immortals to depart, herself abandoned the blood-drenched earth.' Ovid, *Metamorphoses*, Book I, 145.

The explanation would come later, as Zia had entered, saying that another Roman had just knocked at the door, asking for a short meeting – the *subpraefectus classis*[22] himself. It was not his first visit either. The host treated him politely and he was a career military man, past his prime, a man who knew how to adjust his attitude to his interlocutor. Why the soldier was visiting, the young man would not remember and it was not important in the context, anyway. An administrative matter... The proconsul had sent him... Whatever... Too much imperial bureaucracy!

What did remain buried deep in his mind just as a seed that sprouted only then, on that cruel winter night, was the dialogue between the officer and the poet, after Naso apologized that his laugh might have been heard in the street.

'I am glad to find you cheerful, knight Naso! I guess the joke was incredibly good...'

Recklessly, the exiled man decided to play his game.

'My young disciple here, by his name Damanais, Zourdanos's son, believes that there are some lapses in my *Metamorphoses*...'

'Ha! Ha! A bold statement, young man! Can I see what those are?'

Damanais looked at his master inquiringly, and the old man encouraged him.

'Please, Damanais...'

The officer looked over the passage in question, but he did not share the author's enjoyment. Instead, he raised his eyebrows.

'The boy is right. This is not about any iron age, randomly flung who knows when in the history. We both know, knight Naso, that these are recent and regrettable events...'

... And Naso has stopped laughing. Ever since.

---

22 Deputy of the commander of the Roman fleet.

Some time would pass until the young Get found out about the tragic fate for Gaius[23] and Lucius,[24] sons of Marcus Vipsanius Agrippa[25] and the plots made by empress Livia Drusilla… The keys of the past, in verses…

Another night, not long before that bloodied winter, as if he had felt his end was drawing near, Ovid told him to sit next to him. The reddish warmth searing from the hearth was shaping the soft clay of a mood just right for some secret words.

'My child, do not forget your duties. I am not going to leave a will, as I have nothing to leave in it. Whatever was there for posterity, it has already been given. For you, I will entrust you with the task we have talked before. When the time comes, take me to my place. The people you met there, up north, beyond the swamps, will come and help you.'

'How will they know when to…'

'They will. They have their own ways of finding out these things before they even happen.'

'Then, why can't they warn us?'

'Because you might be able to learn your fate, yet you cannot change it. The most important thing is to keep the place secret. Make sure it remains secret even after you breathe your last, until people are able to understand

---

23 Gaius Caesar (20 BC– AD 4), son of Roman general Marcus Vipsanius Agrippa, adopted by emperor Octavian, along his brother, Lucius. Died from a disease, speculated to have been poisoned by empress Livia Drusilla, interested in her son's ascension, Tiberius, hence willing to eliminate any competitors.
24 Lucius Caesar (17 BC– AD 2), son of Roman general Marcus Vipsanius Agrippa, adopted by emperor Octavian, along with his brother, Gaius. He also died from a disease, with the same suspicions as in his brother's demise.
25 Marcus Vipsanius Agrippa (64/62–12 BC), Roman consul, senator, general, architect, good friend of emperor Octavian. Occupied the position of Rome consul twice: 37 BC and 28-27 BC.

exactly what I meant to write on that tombstone. History is going into a certain direction and I am too small to thwart it. One day, people might fathom that history could have been written differently. If I shouted at the top of my voice about what I know or, even worse, wrote a whistleblowing epistle and sent it to Rome, I would not find a hole to hide in and my name, if it survives time, will be associated with the huge scandal that my revelations might create, instead of the verses that have brought me joy and sadness alike. I am not one to tear down. I am one to build up! Through the ages, my testimony will be a source of history, not of war. At least, this is what I hope.'

A long silence followed. Then…

'Listen to me carefully, Damanais! When what will happen anyway happens, run! That's all! Run and do what you have to do!'

And this is exactly what he was doing – running. Or he thought he was. The infernal snow was turning his race into an erratic and sluggish move of despair.

He somehow made it to Diokles's house and started pounding with his fists and feet on the gate. The servants knew him and the master of the house, a man with olive skin and grey hair, who had lost neither the strength of his body nor the sharpness of his mind, despite being older than Naso, was alerted and welcomed him immediately. No need for Damanais to say anything. His simple presence there, in the middle of the night, was much clearer than any orator's speech.

'Guards!' the man yelled.

His trusted men gathered around him and orders started being fired.

'You two rush to Aelius Firmus's house! Naso is a citizen of Rome and it is Firmus's job as a military tribune to deal with this. Tell him to come here, with his guards!

Zenon, you come with me and the Get boy! Tecton, you go to Artemon! You two run to the garrison, on separate ways, and raise the alarm! I want to have men on the walls, don't care about the storm! A killer is on the loose! Call my personal doctor! In the name of Priapus! Where is that Syrian when you need him? I am paying him twice a Dacian shaman and he knows twice less! And, he is lazy, to boot!'

Rolling more than walking, limping on his right leg and hunched like a crone from the bottom of Tartarus, there came the Syrian man...

'Get the oils for the dead!'

Not long after, they reached the house of the killed poet. By the deceased, Zia exhausted of wailing and was crying silently, almost in her mind, a humble weep, accompanied by a litany, neither sung nor spoken, which a layman unfamiliar with the Getae customs could have judged as incoherent. But this is how old Zia had learnt from her ancestors to mollify the demons between the two worlds when they had to welcome a human soul and cross it over. She was speaking their language...

When Aelius Firmus, *tribunus militium augusticlavius*[26] assigned to Tomis on the proconsul's order, walked in shivering and conjuring all the abominations that his mother in Capua, a so-called professional witch, was writing for money on *defixiones*[27] (it was an extensive repertoire!), Ovid's body had already been washed, anointed with aromatic oils and laid on the bed, with the coins for the boatman placed on his eyes. Seeing the still body of his fellow countryman, the officer abandoned his bellicose mood most likely sparked by the fact that he had to leave his warm bed and face the blizzard outside.

---

26 Military tribune of an equester order.
27 Tablets, usually of lead or clay, on which curses were written in the ancient Rome.

He sent his adjutants away quickly.

'It was inevitable,' he concluded, while looking straight at Diokles, who nodded his head and showed towards the wound (now clean) in Naso's chest.

'Killed from a short distance. The blade entered upwards. It pierced his heart.'

The commotion behind the door told them that the archon had arrived. The old Artemon, with his pointy face and grey hair, paler than Ovid, barely breathing due to the effort, even if he had been carried there and had not fought the storm standing on his own feet, which were sinking under him, sat on the chair with difficulty, helped by the servants he sent away afterwards.

'You, slave,' he said to Zia in his raspy voice, after he pulled himself together, 'go and take care of the people waiting over there!'

Zia did not have the willpower to riposte, but Damanais did it for her, in a tone far from friendly.

'She is no slave!'

The old man gestured as… 'Whatever you are saying.'

'Hey, woman, because you are surely one, go away! This is a matter for men! You, too, my child!'

'The child can stay here!' Diokles opposed.

It was the second time those words had been uttered so shortly apart, and the first time had not ended well… But he obeyed the officer's index finger signalling him to stay put. Then, the Roman agreed.

'The child must stay! He is a key deponent. On the other hand, your Syrian has finished his work…'

Diokles dismissed his doctor. The archon, the strategist, the Roman officer, he and Naso's ghost were the only ones left in the room.

'We have to send a letter to the proconsul,' said Artemon. 'And start an investigation.'

'I am sure that the proconsul will be delighted to hear that the man we were supposed to look after was killed right under our noses,' Diokles opined. 'What do you think, Aelius?'

The Roman sighed.

'I think you should have already closed all the exits, at least to make certain the killer is not leaving these walls...'

'Hm,' the military man smiled out of the corner of his mouth. 'I have already done it.'

'Good. Then, an investigation is next... how do these Getae say? Aha! Between us and the wall.'

'And the letter?' the archon insisted.

'Come here!'

The Roman gestured to the strategist and both went closer to the dead body, while the old man was struggling to stand up. Finally, realizing that he would not be able to do it without the help people in there seemed not be bothered with, he settled for stretching his neck, hoping to see the thing the tribune had invited Diokles to study on the corpse – the wound!

'See that? I know this wound. There is only one weapon to leave this behind. It is the *gladius* of the permanent imperial troops. Do you know what this means?'

The strategist frowned. He suspected what that was, but he chose not to articulate his assumptions, that would have meant he accepted the maximum gravity of the situation. The other one would rather say it. And the other one said it.

'It means that Naso's killing was a statement. The man did not hide his identity. He used a Roman weapon, which says he was sent on a mission from Rome, a mission we all expected, to be honest. I believe Ovid was expecting it too, considering his letters and the scene in the peninsula now, with Tiberius the emperor. That simple! The message is "I am a killer paid with Roman money, this is why I came here to do my job with a Roman fighting sword. You should better not meddle in this affair!" This is, of course, for who knows how to read the metaphor in this wound… An ordered murder!'

'So, what do we have to do?' the archon's voice was heard, from behind them.

'Ovid is dead,' said in a dry voice the compatriot of the dead man. 'This is exactly what will be written in the report.'

'And the grave?' the strategist inquired. 'There is only one person who knows where it is.'

Everyone looked at the boy, and he nodded his head,

'And that's how it's going to stay! I will be the only one…'

The tribune made a grimace.

'You are forgetting something – you are the one who knows where it is, but I am aware of what is written on his tombstone. As a military in the pay of the emperor, I cannot approve what is carved on it. It is dangerous for Rome… If made public, the words would bring a vacuum of authority that would throw the entire world into chaos, as Naso himself confessed to me…'

'Augustus would turn in his grave, and Tiberius might come here in person,' the archon bemoaned.

'May all the gods protect you if Tiberius comes here!' Firmus retorted, in a serious voice.

Several moments of silence heavy as the times passed. The proconsul's messenger was taking in the situation. Or at least he was trying to. After Ovid had shown him the incriminated and incriminating text, which he had no doubt was carved on the exiled man's tombstone, he asked Ovid to share the secret with Artemon and Diokles, too. He did not want the whole weight of a situation possibly going haywire solely on his military shoulders. And it could have happened, as the big dilemma crushing him was whether the paid killer had been sent as part of the hunting started by the empress against the former opponents of Augustus and Tiberius, which would have obviously included Naso, based on the epistles sent to Rome through all these years, or something might have been heard about the poet's intention to reveal things not flattering at all about the emperor, which arose the evident need to have him suppressed. One more question – had Ovid kept his promise and told the other two about that text? Until he found an answer, Aelius Firmus was treading on quicksand. He tried to divert their attention from the discussion and threw Damanais to the lions.

'What about the boy? What are we doing with him?'

They all looked at him.

'Ovid is entitled to a grave!' Diokles exclaimed. 'Since this boy is the only one to know the place chosen by Naso for his eternal sleep then I cannot see what the problem might be. Why would we have to do anything specific about him? He should bury his mentor, and be done with it.'

Looking sceptically at the strategist, the tribune, however, insisted, mumbling.

'But, as you already know, the grave will have that stone that…'

The two Greeks in Tomis winked at each other, much to the dread growing on the Roman's face.

'Aah… the inscription!,' went on Artemon, almost amused. 'Well, this is something between you, the Romans. Do you want us to give you assurance that we are going to hold our tongue? All right, we will give it to you. It is not our business, we do not know where the text is, we do not want to meddle in others' affairs.'

'The boy knows even more than we do,' added the strategist. 'Have you taken the oath?'

'Yes,' Damanais admitted, proudly.

'Then, it is all clear. When the Get swears, he will take it with him into the grave. Or to … that Zamolxis of them.'

Aelius Firmus thought that Diokles winked at him, discreetly. Or it was just an illusion he was clinging onto, so he would not lose ground…

*

The storm stopped at dawn. Snow was blanketing the land in a shroud not much different in look and warmth than the one wrapping Ovid's body. Hardly had the day broken when Damanais whipped the horses, while bundled up in warm clothes through the care of Zia, who also had given him enough provisions for the trip. Behind him, in the wagon, the body of his master. The fog swallowed the cart, along with the Get, the dead poet and the horses the moment they had left the main city gate behind. From atop of one of the towers, the strategist and the military tribune were struggling to see something, at least a shadow through the fog curtain, but they could barely see each other, albeit at one foot distance.

'What are we going to do with him?,' asked the Roman.

'We will get him when he comes back.'

Aelius Firmus almost gave a sigh of relief. After all, the strategist's wink from the night before was not an illusion of someone in full panic. The affair with Naso's damn inscription could have ended badly. Diokles and mainly that jackal Artemon had got a half-nelson on him. As it seemed, the poet had kept his promise and told them the secret, too. But many go out for wool and come home shorn. When he had asked Ovid to do it, he reckoned that the secret would unite them, if shared, but not even for a second had he thought that it would be possible to throw the blame on him after the exiled man's demise. In spite of that, Diokles's promise to kill Damanais on his return somehow comforted him. Yes! That was the solution! The young man had to die! Once the only person who knew the site of the grave was removed, the grave itself, along with the body and his inscription, would be buried in history. Even deeper, into the legend.

'I should have sent someone to track him and slit his throat. Then wolves would have covered his tracks. His and Naso's, altogether.'

'Rather risky in this foggy weather. Tribune, you do not have such good men around.'

Under other circumstances, the Roman would have felt offended and have shown it right away. But now, he did not have that luxury... Diokles' friendship, or at least his goodwill, had become more precious that all the gold in the world. He had no desire whatsoever to have to ask for his transfer God knows where. Such things were stirring the suspicions of superiors and they usually ended with a disciplinary transfer to who knows where, Germany or Parthia. At the very least! There was also the variant of demotion or even worse...

'Where do you think the grave is?' Aelius inquired, after a short pause.

'Hm! Right there, beyond the fog,' Diokles answered, pointing to. . nothing.

*

Some time had passed. The fog had lifted. In front of his eyes, white and stretched, with no landmarks other than the sun hanging up in the sky, looking more like a black and perfectly round spot, cut out of the ashy infinity, rather than a star. He knew that, as long as he was keeping it above his left shoulder, the sun, no matter its shape, would lead him where he was supposed to go, because it had its own path and never strayed from it. It had never done it. Why would it do it now, just when it had to guide him on the final journey for the one who had vowed verses to Apollo? The poet had even taken this detail into account. Countless times he had told his disciple that, when his time came, no matter how, the only thing to do was to follow the path of light, from sunup to sundown. The people beyond the swamps were going to do the rest.

After a while, he seemed to spot some little people, in the snow, far in the horizon. And the people were getting bigger. They were waiting exactly where they had to. When he reached them, the people lowered the poet's body and lifted it up to their shoulders. They were the same he had met several years before... A mixed crowd... Roman defectors, Peucini, Scythians, Getae from the right bank of Donaris (most of them), slaves who had escaped, some after they had killed their masters, a few Carpes who had lost their sheep on the way to the Delta for some reasons (they would not talk about it), Roxolani banished from their tribes...

A few of them were carrying the body; behind them, Damanais; followed by the wagon now driven by someone else, and the rest along with them, around fifteen men wrapped in thick fur coats. This is how they walked to the grave.

... And the disciple never went back to Tomis.

Chapter 3
Seven hundred sixty-two
– *Clades Variana*[28]

On the night of Ides of September[29], Lucius Caedicius[30], *praefectus castrorum*,[31] decided for us to leave the refuge in Aliso[32] and go downstream, on Luppia,[33] to Castra Vetera.[34]

He realized we would not have lasted any longer there. Reserves were gone and the fire was spreading quickly from one barrack to another, as most were made of wood. The *castrum* had been abandoned several years before and I am thinking it was only for convenience that Varus[35] had sent

---

28 *Defense of Varus* (Latin) – It is about the clear defense that the Roman armies, led by Publius Quintilius Varus faced against the coalition of German tribes led by Arminius in Teutoburg forest; year 762 ab Urbe Condita means year 9 AD

29 In the Roman calendar, the fifteenth day of the months: Martius, Maius, Iulius and October, but the thirteenth day for the other months.

30 Lucius Caedicius (cca.40 BC–AD 9), high ranking officer with Legion XIX in the Roman army, organized the underground fight of the survivors after the Teutoburg disaster, taking refuge in the Aliso castrum, on Lippe river.

31 In the Roman army at the onset of Empire, the third highest rank of officers, after *legatus* and *tribunus laticlavius*.

32 Roman castrum (probably for summer use) on Lippe river, whose exact location is still under debate.

33 Latin name of the Lippe river in Germany, tributary of the Rhine.

34 Roman castrum located close to the influx of the Rhine with Lippe, city of Xanten in German today

35 Publius Quinctilius Varus (47/46 BC-AD 9), Roman politician and general, defeated in Teutoburg.

him before the bloodbath to patch the fortress at all, for what should have been the last peaceful camp on the 'stroll' to Castra Vetera. A stroll that had cost us much… Yes! It must have been the convenience, not a premonition or the decision of who knows what strategy! He was not putting any value on such things…

The Cherusci[36] of Arminius[37], along with the Sicambri[38] of Deudorix[39], cursed be their names, were pushing the eastern gate of the castrum.

They had been besieging us for three days, after they had pounded on us at *Saltus Teutoburgiensis*.[40] They had probably sworn not to leave any trace of a Roman beyond *Rhenus*,[41] otherwise they would have not bothered to follow us. We were a handful of people, around forty souls that the terror had simply withered away. Among us, almost half were women and children. Nevertheless, we withstood. But for Caedicius's sharp mind, we would have shared the violent death of our comrades. His quick thinking, the cries for help of the hapless who had been captured by the German, still ringing in our ears, the animalic roars of the barbarians on the other side of *Porta sinistra*[42]… Fear of death gives unexpected strength even to the weakest. Women and children had fought side by side with us.

The *Praefectus* called us on *Via principalis*, right next to

---

36 Germanic tribe, led by Arminius, to defeat the Roman armies at Teutoburg.

37 Arminius (cca 16 BC–AD21), son of Segimer, leader of the Cherusci tribe, winner at Teutoburg.

38 Germanic tribe on the right shore of the Rhine, ally of the Cherusci tribe at Teutoburg.

39 Deudorix, son of Baetorix (?-?), leader of the Sicambri.

40 Teutoburg forest (Latin).

41 The Latin name for the Rhine.

42 Porta principalis sinistra, one of the access ways of the standard architecture in the Roman castra.

Praetorium[43] and in his eyes we saw that he had taken a crucial decision and he was ready to share it with us. There were only twelve soldiers left. Well... By 'soldiers', I meant us, the professional legionaries, hardened in the battlefields of Martius. Given the circumstances, the four women and two children surviving the siege had proven worthy of not only being called 'warriors' but of bearing the insignia of a legion. If (or how many of them!) they will have been able to escape from there, may their life be long and peaceful, as they have suffered enough! If not, then... *Sit tibi terra levis!*[44]

We were exhausted, demoralized, famished and the heavy swords were dangling in our hands, more than the shields soaked by rain, which had proven a burden rather than protection a few days before, when we had been ordered to attempt to build a strong place or anything to keep us safe from the barbaric fury. The order has never been fulfilled... The breastplate was slowing me down as it was only holding on two or three buckles. I ripped it off me and for a few seconds I was able to breathe, until my nostrils reminded me of the smoke around and the incandescent air. My legs were injured, but I was too ashamed to lament about it. Women had wounds that had left nothing of their feet, and some human wrecks were carrying children around.

'We are as good as dead here,' Caedicius said in a grave voice, shooting fierce glances over our heads, at the gate hinges barely holding under the barbarians' blows.

He turned around and pointed to the gate on the right.

'We can reach the river quite fast through there. A bit of luck, we might find some boats or at least a bridge we

---

43 Elements of a Roman castrum: Via principalis connected the two gates (left and right), and Praetorium was initially a campaign tent, next a building meant for the commanders.
44 Rest in peace! (Latin).

can cross and lose our trail. Castra Vetera is a few hours away of forced march. We leave now, we have a chance. It is important to understand that everyone is on their own. (A few protested, but the *praefectus* calmed them down with a gesture of concession.) If we are in this situation, it means that we are the last left of Varus legions. No one will come to save us. They would have done it by now. (The blows on the gate were getting stronger and the wood rattling was not a good sign.) But this is something only we know, not the Cherusci. We need to save time. Soldiers! Blow your bugles as if it was for the last time! Blow, because that will be the last thing! Blow, we want the barbarians to think fresh troops have arrived!'

… And this is exactly what we did. The long sound of the military bugles rose from the sea of the flames devouring the fort, as if from the Sundown, where the Germanic had not reached, due to the land, two legions at least had come ready to repel them. For some short seconds, the ram battering stopped. It seemed that Caedicius's plan was working.

'Now!' he ordered, and everyone ran as fast as they could to the exit overlooking the river.

We were running, desperately blowing the bugles. Had we stopped, we knew that the next land we would put our foot on would be the Elysian Fields. Or Tartarus!

And it happened. I heard that long and deep croak. I lifted my eyes to the sky in flames. She was there! Yes! My blackbird, which everyone believed, erroneously, to be a raven and thus gave me my *cognomen*,[45] that very bird landed on the burning roof of one of the buildings on the side, after she had been flying in circles several times.

I froze. Realizing that one of the bugles had gone silent, Caedicius looked over his shoulder. I am trying to

45 The third name, in the conventional system of Roman names, usually a nickname.

remember, but I cannot... It would be hard for me to say if there was any reproach in that look or just a sign that, as everyone was on their own, as far as he was concerned, I could have stopped and taken my fate into my own hands. I believe neither. It might have only been a dangerous temptation, like Orpheus's, on his way out from Inferno. And his Eurydice was called 'Aliso'. Unless his own life was playing Eurydice's role...

As for me, my fate had never been in my hands. It had always been the credit of the black bird. She had saved me from life-or-death situations, guided me in life, my choices were hers and, if I dared to disobey, that would have surely meant my demise. If the black bird was telling me, by the fact she had landed on that roof, to stand still, despite the imminent charge of the Barbarians, then I had to stand still!

I saw them exit and disappear in the darkness. After the short stop, from the other side of *Via principalis*, the blows onto the gate started again, even fiercer than before. As the bugles were no longer heard, the Barbarians figured that everything had only been an attempt of the besieged to gain some time and it was not hard to suspect why. It would have taken them too long to go around the fort and the gate showed signs that it might crack, so they carried on there.

I hid behind a blazing *horreum*,[46] I could barely breathe. Above, through the flames, my black bird didn't seem to care about the inferno around it. It was sitting there on a vane and flicking her head, left to right, as birds do. Her passivity was annoying me. At the same time, the fact that she had taken the decision for me to stay, was giving me hope that we would make it out of there safe.

With a blast like the world had plunged into chaos, *Porta sinistra* gave in and I swear by the memory of my ancestors it was then that I wetted myself. Simple and candid: I

---

46 Barn (Latin).

peed myself! The Sicambri and Cherusci swamped into the castrum and headed like a killer torrent to *Porta dextra*,[47] where my comrades had managed to escape. They paid no attention to sideways or to the flames, which did not bother them much. They only knew one thing – if anyone had left Aliso, then that was the only way they could have taken.

I was trying to hide in the smoke, even if it was giving me terrible head spins. The deep croak of the bird told me it was time we had run, too. She took flight towards south and I ran through wreckage and flames, by the burning barracks, to what used to be *Via sagularis* leading to *Porta praetoria*. I knew that beyond the left gate, the least protected, there were high ramparts that had warded off the raiders for three days. The dirt way rolling out on the other side of *Porta praetoria* was no longer there. It had been closed and abandoned, along with the fortress. There were woods instead. I fathomed that it was going to be an arduous journey, but as usual I put full trust in my black bird. I told her, 'If you really want us to go that way, mother, then so be it!'

And I walked out. I could not know what had come of the other fugitives. I could hear weak screams, in the fire bedlam, but I could not figure out whether they belonged to the Barbarians, they were for intimidation or I should have deciphered horror in them.

My black bird had made a wise decision. No one was following me.

So began my run through the woods of hostile Bructeri and Marsi[48] to *Ara Ubiorum*.[49]

*

---

47   The gate on the right (Latin) of a Roman castrum.
48   Germanic tribes
49   Latin name for the present city of Köln.

My name is Arrius Terentius Corvus, soldier in *Legio Undevigesima Germanica*[50] and this is my story.

I was born during the sixth consulate of Divine Caesar Octavianus[51] and the second of Vipsanius Agrippa, in one of Mediolanum suburbs. My father was a blacksmith and had a small forge shop, with two journeymen. I never met my mother. She died during childbirth. As for my birth, it was surrounded by some unheard things. My mother's death, despite its drama, was not something to have never happened before or ever since. She bled to death and the only thing that midwives could do was to watch her helplessly and pray to the gods. And the gods had mercy on her. They took her away quickly, with no struggle. Not too much. They had mercy on me, too. They gifted me with the black bird. People told me that, right after my mother died, the bird landed on one of the branches of the wild oak growing in our yard and croaked, and I answered with a grunt, as if I talked to, they saw this wonder, many said that the soul of my poor mother had embodied in that feathered creature, which would go with me everywhere. There is some truth in here! Yes! She has come with me everywhere! And, yes! I talk to her. Well, not the same way I talk to people. But I know she is there, I know when she is there and, more than that, I trust her judgment as she has never let me in the lurch in sixty-seven years, not even once. I have been through the darkest hours many times, but she was there. But what people do not know is that my black bird is more than my mother's embodiment. I believe that she also carries my soul. I have been sick, injured and almost left for dead. But I survived. And this is because the life that could have oozed away is not, actually, in me, but in her.

---

50 Legion 19. The moniker of „Germanica' is only for writing purposes, since the real name is not known. It was one of the three legions (XVII, XVIII and XIX) annihilated during the Teutoburg battle.
51 28 BC

Some people wanted to kill her, more or less in jest. Not even the most skilled archers, spearmen or slingshot hunters were able to touch a feather. Instead, they paid a high price for their audacity. Hands dried on one, out of the blue; another one was found the next day with his eyes pecked out... As if the black bird had had, on her turn, someone to take care of her. Some god or some... And I have forged my personality according to her presence – less by self-conservation and more by the idea I am immortal or, anyway, I can defy my fate, since as long as she lives and stays near me, I will live, too.

Her simple presence has brought me the nickname of 'Corvus,' which I am lugging with me... There is nothing I can do! Neither can I say it bothers me, like when I was a little snot! Let's make it clear! My black bird is NOT a raven! In my childhood, I was so obsessed with my *cognomen* that I have studied carefully their entire class and I can say, with full responsibility, that my black bird is NOT a raven! I was a fair-skinned child, not fond of being in the sun. I was not a moor! Nevertheless, they called me 'Corvus'. When I went to school, my first teachers were amazed to hear my nickname. They called my father to explain it to them. To go on a rant here, I have to say yes! I am grateful to my father for having made sacrifices so that I could learn how to write and read – and I am closing then rant here!

When I enlisted, the clerk who was taking my information asked me.

'*Praenomen?*'[52]

'Arrius.'

'*Nomen?*'[53]

'Terentius.'

'*Cognomen?*'

---

52 First name (Latin).
53 Last name (Latin).

'Corvus.'

He looked at me from below his eyebrows, without lifting his head from the papers and looked me down. He laughed.

'Corvus? Ha! Where did you get this, my friend, because I see you are as white as me...?'

I pointed to the bird that was escorting me as usual. She was close to us, on the window sill.

'From her, I answered.

He turned around to see her and got really scared.

'From her? I see it is a he, a raven.'

'She is not a raven, I contradicted him.

'But what is it?'

'She is just a black bird.'

He looked at me, with distrust and pity. In his mind, he had probably given me a diagnosis – I was crazy! Or at least weird...

'Whatever you say, my friend... Whatever... just a black bird... Let's not get angry over such a little thing...'

Anyway... We should not talk too much about a thing! It is not a raven. Ravens are smaller. My bird, with her wings spread out, measures almost seven feet. Their croak has a higher pitch... She croaks like from a long and thick pipe. Even the plumage is different! My bird is blacker than a raven! She is blacker than the darkest nights. She is as black as the formless space before creation.

... Another extraordinary thing happened when I came into this world – I was born with my eyes open! No one would believe me, but I swear I remember my own birth to the last detail. Every contraction pressing upon my temples and squeezing my young bones like straps almost to fracture... Those humours around me and going into my nose, my mouth... Blood! A lot of blood! I learnt its taste even before being nursed to the breast of a merciful lady cook, who had lost her baby less than a month after birth and decided to be my nursing mother. I liked the taste of blood, a bit metallic… Perhaps this is the source of my dexterity in handling the *gladius* to a hasty blood spilling… Yes! The same *gladius* I carried during the German campaign of Tiberius, the one I had in Pannonia where we went to suppress the riots there even though that war should have been against the Marcomanni[54] in Boiohemum[55]… Yes! The same *gladius* that kept me alive in Teutoburg, of which I would not let go, although it seemed much heavier than Sisyphus's boulder while I was running like crazy through the forest of Marsi, as far away as possible from the burnt fortress in Aliso.

If the body of a grown man were put under the same pressure a newborn has to go through at birth, it would surely snap! Every muscle, every tendon, every bone is pushed inside of you and the lungs, which still have no clue why they are there, contract until you feel like the air is being sucked out of you to the last drop, the same air brought in by the liquid that had been your home but has now turned into deluge, coming out of the womb alongside you! And I have seen all of these!

My father was told I was a marked man. Maybe this is why he sent me to school. Poor him, he departed us to join his ancestors in the consulate year of Nero Claudius Drusus Germanicus,[56] when I was a novice soldier in *Undevigesima*, back then stationed in *Ara Ubiorum*. And he died still waiting to prove my 'marking'. To be honest, I was waiting, too. Until then, the only thing I had been doing was to survive.

---

54 AD 6; The future emperor Tiberius started the fight against the Marcomanni, German population, but the riots of the tribes in Pannonia diverted the campaign.
55 Ancient name for Bohemia, coming from the tribes of Boii living there.
56 Nero Claudius Drusus Germanicus (38 BC–9 BC), Roman general and politician, adoptive son of Octavianus and brother of future emperor Tiberius; also, the father of the future emperor Claudius.

But if the gods bore with me and my black bird saw it fit to take me through the life maze, I must be meant for something special… Something that I could still not fathom, since my abilities were rather limited – I was a soldier and knew how to wield the sword to kill, but as long as I had served under the legion flag, I had never done it with a purpose other than to keep myself alive. It is something that now, in my old age, when writing these words, I wish I could have refused.

Now that the conversation has turned to my life, the very life I was running for on the night when I escaped Aliso, while tree branches were scratching my face, it is best to say that it has been a constant fight since my early years. Besides the fights with the other children, who were having a roar about my *cognomen* that clashed with my skin tone, taunting me however it struck them, I had to wage another battle, this time much harder, the battle with myself.

One year after my mother's death, my father married again. A butcher's daughter, she was a good woman, healthy, with a bit of a dowry. Not once did she want to replace my mother or get rid of me, as it often happens. She was a gentle woman who minded her business. Three years later, she gave birth to a girl, my half-sister, Servillia. She even survived the birth, which made me, a foolish child, hate her a bit Only a bit, since I had the black bird, anyway. But Servillia was simply adorable! Since her first months of life, I took on the role of her protector as well as her toy. I was like those big, fluffy dogs whose fur children pull on with an innocent cruelty that doesn't bother them one bit, on contrary, they will challenge the children to do it again and guard them from any harm, only to have them play as cruelly and innocently as usual. I was Servillia's fluffy dog.

But she was growing, I was growing, too… In time, that brotherly, protective love turned into something else. For her part, Servillia changed her stock of touches, words and looks. I was no longer a toy. Actually, I think it was her who, consciously or not, initiated the transformation, and I just followed her lead. Not looking for excuses. There is no reason to apologize for the feelings we had for each other, all the more that we were half siblings on our father's side only. Besides, we did not go farther than some harmless kisses and equally naive touching. Yet there was so much quivering in her svelte figure, like that of a young feline, so much desire in her eyes and in the lips she was biting to the brink of pain anytime I was around her! This is the fight I fought against myself!

These things did not escape the attention of our parents. They wanted to marry her off to a cloth merchant, a fat and drooling old man who seemed to take off a thick layer of lard whenever he wiped the sweat off his bald head. Luckily, the lecherous character died in time, before they consummated the marriage. He may have simply burst from too much food he had been gobbling up – one day, he was found with his entrails hanging out, pecked on by who knows what bird might have happened to fly around there…

They thought they should bring us apart, somehow… And they sent me to pursue a military career. Now I realize that, in my eighteen years of soldiering, which were bearing down on me while I was running like crazy through unknown woods, I had only seen my sister three or four times. We wrote many letters to each other, it is true, but I was sure that I would have not recognized her. I thought she might have married, after all, and had kids… I wanted a beautiful life for her! All the best things in a world that has nothing to offer. But it hurt! It hurt in a way that not even my black bird was able to console. I started thinking that if I stayed alive I would look for her. But I would back off if my presence made her uncomfortable.

As for my military training, it was hard, that's common

knowledge… We were training to march twenty miles a day, carrying the *pilum*,[57] shield, *gladius*, breastplate and the *sarcina* on our back… But that sense of pride bringing you under the legion Aquila when you see it lifted up, on top of the pole adorned with *phalerae*,[58] or that changes the effigy of the legion, in our case the Capricorn,[59] into a symbol you almost worship, the blood boiling in your veins when the centurion or maybe the commander himself gives an inspiring speech before the fight, all these make the hard training turn into a distant dream. Not even a nightmare… A… nothing…

Even though I had never held a *gladius* in my hand before enlisting (except for the wooden ones I was playing with in my childhood), it seemed the sword was a natural extension of my arms. My art (I can call this skill 'art' and believe me, my dear reader, I am not blowing my own trumpet!) did not pass unnoticed. This is how I started serving the stindard of S.P.Q.R.[60] in the first cohort, under the direct command of Marcus Caelius,[61] *Primus Pilus*,[62] a proud man, coming from Bononia,[63]

---

57 Spear (Latin).

58 Golden, silver or bronze discs, decorated with various motives, which could have been carried on either the breastplate like medals (in case they were granted to individual soldiers for special merits), or placed in full view, on the support of the legion aquila, when this legion was awarded such distinctions as a military unit.

59 License. The emblem of Legion XIX is not known.

60 Senatus Populusque Quiritium Romanorum (Latin) – Senate and people of Rome.

61 Historic character, (cca 45 BC–AD 9), a primus centurion of Legion XVIII, annihilated at Teutoburg. Even though he served in a different legion other than the fictitious character Arrius Terentius Corvus, his bringing into the narrative line exclusively serves with the historicity nature of the story.

62 Primus centurion, commander of the first cohorts of each legion, career military and counselor of the senator-ambassador.

63 Ancient name for Bologne.

who had passed his prime with that refinement only people at peace with themselves show. *Triarius*[64] Caelius was such man. He had fought in many campaigns, amassed a large fortune. For him, the war was no longer a job or the occasion to 'legally' plunder the conquered lands. He understood the war from its political perspective, in the sense that Rome would not able to justify its role in history, in the absence of war, no matter how much harm it brought. Such an idea came along with the assumption of his own role in this large orchestration. Marcus Caelius could proudly call himself an 'artist in the ensemble of the imperial arms of service.'

I will spare you my feats of arms during Tiberius's campaigns. Why? A simple answer. I am sure a lot of ink has been spilled about them. But I would like to revisit the disaster at Teutoburg, since I doubt there are many to have survived it, to tell stories about it. And there is something else... I am an old man. My *gladius* is resting in a reliquary and waiting for me to join it, which will probably happen soon. At one time, I met, briefly, a man who was saying that his weapon was the word. I am writing now. I am using his weapon, even though I have favoured the veracity of iron my whole life. Yes! The word is a weapon but also an elixir for people have lived enough... Telling the story about the defeat at Teutoburg means, for me, to pluck the ones worthy of eternal glory from the clutches of death as well as my way of cursing the ones who pushed my brave comrades over the edge of oblivion.

From the very beginning, I have to admit that had the three legions been under the command of Tiberius or Germanicus, the disaster could have been avoided. I can confess that now, since I am an old man, with nothing to lose and far away from a Rome that has more serious things

64 Roman career military, usually veteran, aged and wealthy.

to worry about now with the madness of the new emperor, Caligula! Yes! I can say it now! Even though Varus's ineptitude led to the Teutoburg massacre, it was not his fault! You cannot blame a dog for barking or biting, this is what he does! This is his job! But what you can do is admonish the dog master, for not keeping him on a leash! It was solely the fault of the man who named him the commander of the army on the Rhenus! Octavian Augustus himself! Varus was a dreamer from a military standpoint. He had been a proconsul in Syria, had actually done a good job there, from what I heard. And this is because he was probably a good administrator in times of peace. Of peace! Octavian's guilt was to not have understood that the Germanics were not the Syrians. The Syrians had been living for some time within the empire borders, had grown accustomed to the idea, were sophisticated, their will had been broken, while the Germanics still had theirs. Their blood was boiling! Actually, I do not think it was blood running through their veins, but fire!

Moreover the man whose friendship he valued so much, Arminius, raised and educated in Rome, was originally a Germanic prince and had not for a second forgotten it!

On that fateful day, five before the Ides of September,[65] we set off for Castra Vetera. Since Varus thought it would only be a pleasant stroll into the countryside, to the twenty thousand plus soldiers, we had women joining (with everything else related to their presence, such as trading, house chores, family or concupiscence), children, convoys with provisions, even siege weapons, useless as they would have been in case of need… It seemed more like a… large-scale picnic. Arminius had blabbered something about riots in the north, but it was also him who had implied that a full display of the imperial force would have been enough to

---

65 8 September, year IX.

dishearten anyone. And while we were at it, why take one legion only? Let us take three! Finally, why should we not let it be understood that our true strength comes from the relaxation with which we are exerting our right (!) to rule the world? In other words... let us be relaxed!

Along with a few horsemen, Lucius Caedicius was sent ahead, to check the shelter in Aliso. Even if Castra Vetera was not very far, there was no point in tiring ourselves... We were going to spend the night there...

This did not bode well with some people though. Marcus Caelius had given fair warning that our narrow column, stretching over many miles, would enter a mountainous area where our ranks would become even narrower and cavalry would not be able to spread out and defend our flanks. Despite being a respected military man, his superiors dismissed him. Some of Varus's relaxation or irresponsibility had rubbed on them... Woe to the commander who thinks he is safe! He did not even catch on when the people of the Cherusci man diverted him from the initial route, taking him on what seemed (too late, though!) a parallel shoulder of the road, built so as to constrict his movements and hide battle ready warriors behind it. Conveniently, Arminius vanished in the falling fog, allegedly, to check on the rearguard. Then, it started raining. It was pouring spitefully, sluicing with hatred, as if to confirm that ominous lighting which was said to have hit the Temple of Mars in Rome, sometime before.

Our feet were sinking in mud up to the knees and so were the wheels of the wagons, making our advance almost impossible.

Despite orders, Marcus Caelius told us to march in the most compact alignment possible. As much as the ground would allow us. His soldier instinct had told him that there was something putrid, other than the wet wood of the trees or the stench reaching us from the swamps farther up north.

Three legions, six cohorts and three alae, plus *auxiliae* and a convoy, everyone was dragging ahead like a sick snail. Hiding in the heights, among trees and behind the shoulder they had built, the Barbarians might have been looking at us, waiting for us to get tired because of our mulish wagons. They did not need to wait too long... First, news from the head of the column. Nothing to worry about... Several attacks, more like a hassle, with a clear target – the convoy with provisions.

More than incompetent in grasping what was really going on, Varus sent the *auxiliae* there, not picking up on the fact that they were mostly warriors from the so-called pacified Germanic tribes! Guess what? They all deserted. What a surprise!

We were ordered to build a stronghold, as it was obvious we would not be able to advance any further. Neither would we be able to build a shelter over the night, as we didn't have where! We were between the woods and the ravine. We spent the night there, hiding only under our shields, which would be rendered useless in battle anyway after having soaked up the rain. The situation was not extreme, though. It was quite normal to be afraid in the darkness, the rain and the fog, with news travelling through the ranks, being distorted from ear to mouth and from mouth to ear, and the battle noises escalating and going down from where the Barbarians were attacking. Not an imminent danger, yet. For us, at least, as we were in the head of the column. I would make too much of it to compare the feeling we had then with what you felt right before a battle, when your heart sticks into your throat, like a stone shot from a sling and your brain drains of all your thoughts or any trace of humanity and you are on the verge of becoming either a predator, or a hand of dust. No! It was more like a discomfort, somehow augmented by the worry I could read on

Caelius' face. Was he really the only sober man in a crowd of drunks?

From time to time, I would move away the shield on top of my head, trying to spot the black bird. To no avail! It was night and there was also a thick fog! She was probably flying somewhere, above the clouds, scrutinizing not only the land but also the future.

It was still raining in the morning. Varus was unshakable. The reports, far from being realistic, (one could not ask for more, given the weather conditions), were talking about minor losses. The commander was still sure that the harassment of the rearguard of column was nothing more than a tolerable echo of the alleged riots that our simple march should have squashed. For him, that march was still just a saunter! Not even the ,mysterious' disappearance of Arminius raised a question. Or the warnings of Sagestes,[66] possibly the only Germanic leader still loyal...

At that moment, they stormed upon us! Cherusci, Bructeri, Sicambri, Marsi, Chasuari, Angrivari, over fifteen thousand warriors, hideous to look at, screaming from the top of their lungs. They seemed to have been dislodged from the very mountains they were tumbling down on, like a destructive avalanche. The only thing Varus did was to send a patrol to gather information. No one came back.

We were not able to fight the way we had been trained. The force of the legion was in its cohesion and our weapons had been invented to turn a mass of people into a killer monolith. Our large, rectangular shields served precisely this purpose, but they were a burden in a one-on-one fight. And we had to fight like that! No other choice!

The surge of Barbarians would not stop coursing through our lines, which were incapable of fighting back as the room needed for manoeuvring was completely missing.

---

66 Arminius's uncle.

With each new wave of spears, axes, war hammers, maces, swords, hatchets, our numbers were thinning. And the black bird was nowhere to be seen...' Have you forsaken me, mama?'

To my right, Bricius, a Helvet[67] from *Agri Decumates*,[68] was cursing on all the Gal and Roman gods together. He had wanted to get the citizenship and this was the price he was now paying for that! He died uttering something quite unflattering about the Great Mother of all gods when a Cherusci axe threw half of his head several meters away. On the other side, legionary Rufus Philo, along with his *cacula*,[69] was struggling to turn his shield into a barricade in front of a red-haired hulk that had lifted his huge hammer above his head, getting ready to strike them. In vain! The hammer passed through the soggy shield like a knife through butter, levelling the soldier and his servant to the ground. From the right of Philo, Furius, one of my people in Mediolanum, whom I used to share memories about my birth place, stuck his *pillum* between the hulk's ribs. The redhead staggered, fell on one side, yet still had some time to hit Furius in his chest with the hammer, cramming the cuirass into his ribs, and the latter into his heart. I swooped then with my *gladius* onto him and I stabbed him deeply between his neck and his collarbone. He shot a glance at me, so terrible that I feared he would stand again and hit me with that heavy hammer. He never got the chance. I ripped the blade from him and cut his head. Barbarians were infernal demons. No sooner had you thought you mowed down one then two or four more were popping up and that went

---

67 Member of the Helvetii tribe, Celtic of nation.

68 A region of the Roman Empire to comprise Raetia and Germania Superior, between the Black Forest Mountains, the Rhine and the Danube.

69 Servant, slave of a soldier.

on and on. It was disheartening… And we were feeling our strength draining out with every blow we barely avoided or thwarted.

Our cohort ceased to exist when Marcus Caelius fell. The two freedmen, Privatus and Thiaminus,[70] who accompanied him everywhere, tried in vain to get him out of the commotion where he had died, pierced by five Barbarian spears. They died, too, along with their master. The lieutenant attempted to gather us but there was no chance. His horsehair-adorned helmet flew away, along with the head in it, after a Cherusci I recognized as one of Arminius's men, hit him right in the middle of it with the axe. Carving that Barbarian, that tremor, the shudder of the flesh when the *gladius* plunged in it made me feel a pleasure next to ejaculation, as I knew my sword had sunk into a traitor's chest. After the lieutenant's death, the first cohort of the legion, which should have had the most disciplined soldiers, turned into a pool of blood, entrails, flesh, bones and scraps of weapons under the reeling blows of the Germanics.

That could hardly be called a 'fight'…

Darkness came again and most of us just waited for the final blow. We could not see anything around. We could hear something but did not know what that was. The rumour that Vala Numonius, Varus's *legatus*, tried to escape to the swamps in the north, but was caught and whacked, just flew by us, like it was not our matter. Actually, it was not! We were only worried about those incandescent eyes, seemingly coming from Tartarus, because everyone knew that once they entered their sights, they would be as good as dead.

In the morning, when even the demons had to rest for a while, we were ordered to abandon our positions. We were

---

70 Historic characters, freedmen of Marcus Caelius, pictures on his cenotaph.

about to leave the convoy and the wounded behind. The women and children who were able to follow us, were free to do it or face certain death! We were supposed to make a breach somewhere, towards west, at the gorge exit, and set up a defensive camp. It was only after we had managed to somewhat gather ourselves, that the extent of the devastation became clear. We were left with almost no cavalry. It would have been useless anyway on such a terrain. Returned from Aliso, Lucius Caedicius had under his command little over a dozen of horsemen. The *scorpios* and ballistae we had been carrying with us just to 'impress' the rebels had been the first to fall. The soldiers manning them were next, unable to defend them. The bowmen had also bitten the dust. We, the survivors, were bearing the horrible marks of the attacks. Almost all of us had dumped our shields. A stench of raw meat was making our stomachs turn.

We could barely count five or six cohorts. Plus women and children, kept alive by the gods solely for their own amusement. We knew that whatever we were about to do was suicidal, but we did it anyway! We tried to break the blockade, even though over twenty thousand warriors had not succeeded in doing that, so it looked almost impossible for three thousand mangled soldiers in shreds. And Varus knew that! This is why he killed himself, along with all his generals. I came to the conclusion that suicide was a futile luxury, since death came anyhow. He was there, busy! I could see him, up close even, as Barbarians would fight long and with all their might, sleeping in short, deep bouts that quickly made them fresh and ready for bloodshed again. Hammers were pounding on us, as if we were nails to be knocked into wood, and axes were striking us down like stalks.

It was then that I ran! Not afraid to admit it. I ran because I saw my black bird flying to Aliso. Others followed me, some only to lose their life on the ramparts of the abandoned castrum, a few trying to save theirs while escaping with Caedicius.

Barely making it to Ara Ubiorum, after a four-day mad run through the woods, only feeding on the image of the black bird flying above my head, I found out that a few you could count on the fingers of one hand had managed to get away and sound the alarm. Somehow, someone had reached Mongontiacum,[71] and general Lucius Nonius Asprenas, Varus's nephew, had deployed the First Legion Germanica and the Fifth Legion Alaudae, to occupy Ubiorum and Castra Vetera to secure the *limes*[72] on Rhenus.

As for me, I had decided that my adventure as a legionary was to end right there and then. I could have covered my traces easily. They could have declared me dead. I had not given any thought to how I was going to return home and find Servillia, without the money I ought to have earned as a veteran. The only thing I knew was that, had I reported to any unit I would have had to serve for several more years before I was financially stable enough to carry out my plan. But I had seen death… up close. So… I had had enough, thank you very much! Despite the flaws in my sense of self-preservation, something was telling me that the black bird, which was still watching me, could not put me on equal footing with the gods. And her long and deep croak assured me that my reflection was accurate.

I shed everything connected to my legionary life, including the strip of skin on my shoulder where I had tattooed the Capricorn of the legion and its number; I only saved my sword and some rags, so I will not walk naked into the city, and I blended in with the poor swarming on the streets in Ara Ubiorum.

---

71 Ancient name for the current city Mainz (Germany).
72 Border.

Chapter 4

Seven hundred sixty-seven
– Sometime, around the Ides of June

Naso got off his horse. It had been a long journey, but it did not seem to have tired him too much. He had confessed to the Get that it was not the first time he had been travelling past the channels, the swamps and the fog, north of Histria. The first time he had come here with Dionisodor, Crispus and some other people from the merchant's household. And the reason was culinary. While visiting his good friend, the poet had tasted something that initially seemed repulsive, but then he had to admit to have been the most refined delicacy that his Roman tongue, used to the finesse of the food served to the refined people in the capital of the world, had ever tried. They looked like blackberries the host had served after he had preserved them in oil and salt. He found out, actually, they were not fruit but sturgeon roe. Then, Dionisodor invited him to see the source of that wonder. This is how he ended up meeting the locals of that province seemingly out of this world, where people coming from nations that would normally fight against one another, were living peacefully in one place. It was a world of outcasts, brought together by their very proscriptions. They were living their life at the same pace with the fish they were catching and the game they were hunting. They knew when the mating season of all species happened and they would respect their intimacy with an almost religious strictness, as they were aware that they would endanger their lives in the long run, had they disturbed the animals on the land, in the water or air while the latter were doing their duty to the species. They were hunting and fishing as much as needed, with no waste. They were selling from the fruits of their labour, not to get rich but rather to procure what they were missing, especially because they did not have the best land for agriculture. They were living on small islands in the middle of the channels, where they had built wooden huts, lined with clay and furs and covered in the straw found in abundance around.

The tribe of twenty people had adopted the Roman knight banished from his country, even if his visits to their land were not that frequent. They felt kindred with him because of his expatriation and saw him as one of their own kind, the feeling being mutual.

They were not bandits. Some had erred towards their own folk and were hiding, others had decided to leave from who knows what urban agglomerations, a few had escaped from slavery. They had not ganged up to loot, but rather they came together to share a life in the peace of which they had been deprived because of their own doing, of others' or nobody's, before settling in the delta of the great river.

The one who seemed to be the leader was called Tertius Valens, a burly man born and raised on the outskirts of Baetica,[73] in a *vicus*[74] no far from Abdera,[75] the last born in a poor family of fishermen. The youngest, but seemingly the most audacious... He had enrolled in the imperial army and, after a while, he was promoted to a rank, albeit inferior, but enough to imagine himself being able to go higher. He

---

73 Baetica, Roman province in the Iberian Peninsula.
74 Village (Latin).
75 City in Baetica province.

had been a *tesserarius*[76] in the Fifth Legion Macedonica. But nobody is perfect. Tertius Valens had one bad habit – drinking. And it was the drinking that got him in trouble. The legion had been in the Oescus[77] *castrum* for some time... Soldiers were spending their time doing military drills, shooting dice... Drabness. There was no lack of women or wine either. It was like being on holiday. Once in a while they were clashing with the Dacians to the left of the river, when they were coming down, mainly in winter, on an ice bridge, to steal from the villages on the right bank of the Danubius and a bit southward. But no one could call this 'war'. Tertius Valens had just received his rank, entrusted with the night guards, and it seemed that advancement had gone to his head. He had thought that, since a small potato like him, from the other side of the continent, had ranked up in the military hierarchy (albeit a bit), then only a few small steps would separate him from being an emperor. And if you mix this empty illusion with the wine... it leads to nothing good. In his case, it turned into an altercation with one of the centurions who had unwittingly ordered something to Valens of all people, who was already intoxicated on the rank and the wine and therefore saw himself as the ruler of the world.

The centurion wound up on a one-way ride on Charon's cruise boat and Valens, instantly sobered up by the murder he had just committed, deserted. Right on that fateful night, without hesitation, he mounted the first horse he could find and off he went! He rode along the river downstream, galloping the horse to death. He was caught by robbers and barely escaped alive, ending up in a land no one seemed to

---

76   Inferior rank in the Roman army, tasked to organize the night watch.
77   Roman *castrum* in the south of the Danube. Today, locality of Ghighen, in Bulgaria.

have set foot on before. He reckoned he should stay there. It seems that others too, while running away from their past, had thought the same once they got to that beautiful, strange land, dazzling yet fraught with danger, an expanse with waters ebbing and flowing as if they had a mind of their own, an empire of crude green, crystal blue, but also of inscrutable mist or hoary winters.

One way or another, the refugees of this enchanted land had turned it into their home, not only because it was distant from a past that could have haunted them or on account its inaccessibility, but also for the sake of those contrasts, the extremes which mirrored their own destinies and stories, with their ups and downs. It was there, and only there, that their destinies and stories could metamorphose into legends that would enrich the place and endure through the ages.

He was not the only deserter in the group, even if not all of them were Romans or had left the imperial armies. A Get, called Derzis, very knowledgebase about the healing herbs, had been in the army of some minor king to the left of the Danubius but he had fled the camp his lord had ordered to set up after a part of the army had rebelled, stirred by a usurper to the throne.

One of them, who seemed to be Valens' lieutenant, called himself 'Gnur, the son of water' and he was a Scythian. He was boasting that a long time ago, in his childhood, he was told he had been saved from the river Borysthene[78] by a slave, thus being given the name of 'the son of water'. He was a man of few words, but appreciated for his hunting skills.

There were also Asphartes, the Roxolani who claimed to be of noble birth but had been chased away from his people occupying the lands north of Dinogetia,[79] for the

---

78 Dnieper.
79 Dacian-Gaetian settlement, situated on the left bank of the Danube, close to the confluence with Siret.

crime of not having agreed to an arranged marriage to the daughter of a nearby ruler for a political alliance; Solon, the Greek slave with a grand name, escaped from the house of a ship owner in Tyras[80] for reasons he would never talk about and the others would never question; Lucius Laurianus and Septimius Macer, Roman *milites*[81], also deserters; the brothers Davos and Mucaporus, Dacians who had come down from the mountains five years before, shepherding some herds of sheep that were supposed to spend the winter somewhere in the fields but never reached them – and the two would seal their lips every time people mentioned transhumance…

One Carpi was reading the stars. He was telling the other when to sail on the channels and when the high tide was coming. Gnut knew when the storm was coming or not, only from hearing the frogs croak. Another one was searching the stars to find the line and meaning of life and time and the stars were talking back to him. One of the former slaves was cooking a fish soup so tasty that the alleged Roxolani prince and two or three cronies could have sworn that, one night, they had seen Hermes himself stealing a ladle of that unbelievable food. They each had their own story…

He had got to know almost everyone, and they were open with him. People had borrowed customs and beliefs from one another. They had mixed their languages so much that the way they were communicating could be easily deemed as a new language. They had a few yet clear rules – a severed hand for theft, death for death of a man. And everyone was still in one piece. Only one time did they execute a man. It had happened not long after Tertius Valens had joined the group. That single example was sufficient to discourage anyone inclined to spill the blood of any tribe member.

---

80   Greek colony in the north-west of the Black Sea.
81   Foot soldiers in the Roman army.

*

That summer of the year seven hundred sixty-seven since the founding of Rome, when the exiled poet along with his Get disciple had arrived in the village of the outlaws, the former *tesserarius* welcomed them, with his bear-like waddle.

'Always a joy to have you here with us, honourable Publius Ovidius Naso!'

The visitor hugged him, smiling. When Damanais dismounted, he did not receive the same greeting. On the contrary, the deserter shot him a distrustful look. Not taking his eyes off him, he spoke to the poet.

'Crispus, what happened to him?'

'He died, sadly,' he answered, in a sad voice. 'Last winter... an attack... an arrow with the head dipped in snake poison...'

'Well... The Bastarnae are known to do this...'

'Not only them. There were Gets as well. The 'good' habits travel fast. But gods made it so that the Gets who took my good Crispus gave me the young Damanais you see here, in exchange.'

Tertius Valens continued to look askew at the boy. He called out Davos's name and gestured for him to come closer.

'He is one of yours, from the lower plains...'

Davos grinned, showing his all-black teeth, and set to his task. He spit a question to the boy, in his language.

'Who's your family?'

,My father is Zourdanos, he is a farmer. My mother's name is Zura.'

Davos mumbled an ,ahmm,' then he turned to Tertius Valens, signalling with the look in his eyes that the boy was fine.

'Please, forgive me, gentle knight,' he apologized to Naso,

'but you can never be vigilant enough. It seems that your servant speaks with the correct accent. You know, sometimes we have people coming here with impure thoughts, that just want to infiltrate among us and then rat on us to the rulers They come, we expose them, they try to run away, we catch them, and the eddies of god Danubius finish them up... Quite dangerous these waters...'

Ovidius thought it was funny, Damanais not so much, as he was keen on clarifying his status.

'I am not a servant. I am his disciple.'

Tertius Valens allowed an admiring look to show on his face.

'Look at that! He knows Latin, too.'

He put his hands on Ovidius's shoulders and invited him to his hut. The young Get was taken over by his 'cousins' from the mountains, to be introduced to the others in the community.

It was a memorable evening, with the fire spiralling up in the sky, the fish soup adored by the god of robbers, bawdy songs, which the classy poet seemed to truly enjoy... All in all, but there was something in that salty air that you could only find there... The perception of absolute freedom... The starry sky, the nice breeze, the toads croaking, even the annoying mosquitoes barely repelled by the smoke...

Ovidius was lying on the wet ground, his hands under his head, intensely breathing in that dark infinity. Not very far, by the fire, Damanais was singing along with the others. The brass *rhyton*[82] in his hand contained both the source of his good mood and the premonition for the hangover of the next day. The sound of approaching footsteps could have startled him anywhere, anytime but there... Tertius Valens came close.

'You can't find a night like this at Tomis, right?'

---

82   In ancient times, a conical vessel of metal or china, in the shape of an animal horn

'So true,' the knight agreed.

The deserter lay down next to him, propping his jaw in his palm.

'There is no exile here, because we have the infinity. Exiled are the others, with their edicts, treason, poison, and yes! With all their wealth... Augustus himself is a poor man, prisoner in a golden cage. With all the conspiracy against him, around him, I pity him.'

'Had you thought the same a few years ago, you would not have had the dreams of greatness that brought you here.'

'Yes, so true! I could have been an *aquilifer*[83]...'

They shared a hearty laugh.

'To be more serious now, knight Naso, the only thing I sincerely regret is the centurion's wasted life. He was a nice man. He had a wife and a child, somewhere in Calabria... The demons in the inferno set him on my path that night.'

The poet sighed.

'Yes, it was precisely them, the demons of the inferno and those of the libation,' stressed Tertius Valens, his gaze hooked up somewhere among the constellations hanging in the sky.

They kept quiet for a few moments, not necessarily in tribute to the centurion. Sometimes, silence is just silence and nothing else.

'It was meant to be,' the deserter spoke again. 'The same as you were fated to know both glory and disgrace... It took the loss of a life to understand that... Why so? No idea. Gods' ways are different from ours; this is why they are gods. Augustus built an empire and he is captive in it. I killed a man and I am freer than the ruler of the world. Look! See that star?'

He pointed to a random spot in the sky. Ovidius nodded his head.

'If I want, I can hold it between my fingers.'

---

83 Roman soldier of an inferior rank, bearer of the legion acquila.

Squinting one eye, as if aiming at a target, he extended two fingers to the sky, as if he was pinching the distant star. It was a nice game, an interesting optical illusion. But the star moved. For a second, it looked like a candle, flickering against a strong wind. Then, it was out.

'It's died,' Ovidius concluded. 'Or maybe it died a long time ago and we have not seen it until now…'

'Yes. It is exactly what I told you, gods do things differently. Why would they make me pick that exact star? It could have been any other one. There are heaps up there. Was not it enough that I killed a man? Now, I have killed a star, too.'

'Fate…'

'What is yours?'

'To survive my death through my creation.'

'And until then?'

Ovidius raised himself on one elbow and looked straight at his interlocutor, suddenly interested.

'Where are you going with that?'

The other one smiled.

'Nowhere else. I am already here, in the place where killing a star means poetry, no matter if it had been dead before or not. If it was dead, then it happened in its world, not ours, somewhere far away. For us though, it died exactly a few seconds ago, the star or the memory of its image, floating like a phantasm through the universe, all the way down to us. All that matters is the poetry in a star's death.'

'My exile is in Tomis,' said Ovidius, in a dry and sad voice.

The deserter shook his head.

'Wrong, my dear knight… Totally wrong! Your exile is here!'

And he poked him with the index finger in his chest, over his heart, to clear that up.

For a while, they looked at the cheer around the fire, in silence. A sign of freedom...

'And what should I do then?,' the poet asked after some time.

'Hm, do what you wrote that others did– metamorphose yourself!'

'Into what?'

'Into something that will get you out of yourself, out of Tomis or the intrigues in Rome and bring you here. Don't you understand how small the empire is compared to the rest of the world? Which is better? To be free in a cage or captive in the vastness of the universe? I am giving you the universe...'

Tertius Valens got up, giving him a friendly pat on his shoulder and left him alone with his thoughts. And those thoughts kept him awake late after the fire had gone out and the party people had already fallen asleep.

The next day, after he bought the fish roe and the fish for which he had taken this trip (how many times before?) and the Roxolani made sure that the goods were strapped tight on the back of the donkey they had borrowed from the Histrian merchant, the poet said goodbye to Tertius Valens. Damanais was clumsily pretending to be on his best behaviour. Actually, he had a splitting headache. He was barely able to mount his horse, to the quiet amusement of the others.

'Poor boy,' exclaimed Asphartes, while checking the straps on the donkey.

'And what is it going to be, my poet?' the former *tesserarius* enquired, in a playful tone. 'Are we going to metamorphose ourselves or not, for the sake of freedom?'

'How could I do that?' asked Ovidius, while mounting on his horse.

'Use your imagination! You are the poet, aren't you?'

Naso grabbed the reins, getting ready to leave.

'So long, my friend!'

The other man smiled in the corner of his mouth and saluted with a slight nod.

'Farewell, my knight! Next time we see each other, let's be free together!'

The journey to Histria was longer, for the simple fact that silence stretches the distance, as much as the words shrink it. One of them was quiet as his noggin was hurting like hell, while the other one was just following the deserter's advice – using his imagination.

*

Dionisodor was a perceptive fellow. Nothing got past him. Well... The thoughts having tortured Naso for... miles on end, were not so difficult to pick up on, especially for someone like him. Sunken cheeks, eyes barely open... Visits to Tertius Valens's 'empire' were no reason for the fatigue to leave such marks. But the poet's face was saying something and no words were needed to attest to that!

The merchant ordered the people to unload the goods off the back of the donkey and led his friend into the house. His *oikia*[84] was exquisite, with two upper-stories, slender Ionic columns, capitals with volutes like ram's horns and richly adorned friezes, creating the impression of floating, amplitude and perfect proportions, not only due to the volumes but also for the bright white of the marble, with discrete hues of pink and emerald.

The host gave the travelers enough time to freshen up and take a rest. One skilful slave (who was called Hygeia,[85] believe it or not, whatever her real name was!) was tasked

---

84 Housing for single family, in ancient Greece.
85 Goddess of good health, ancient Greeks.

to bathe Ovidius and give him a relaxing massage. For the honour guest, they had prepared the *caldarium*[86] with polychrome mosaic above the *hypocaust*.[87] The water in the bath, heated to just the right temperature, smelled of lavender, while warm steam puffs carrying soothing aromas were coming through the holes carved in the wall. Hygeia, an olive-skinned, ebony-haired Bythinian had golden hands and Ovidius yielded to the will of those hands through which deities themselves seemed to be working. But Hygeia had something more – piercing eyes and full lips of an almost naughty red, breasts like hard apples, firm and warm thighs, full of promise. And Ovidius bowed again, poor old man…

Back with the mortals, Naso was dressed in a soft, elegant *himation*, embroidered with colourful stripes and clasped over the shoulder with a fibula, then he was perfumed and invited to choose his jewellery, after the Greek custom.

His Romans were more austere, but he had mingled with the elite, and was no stranger to jewels. He picked a golden hair pin, with rubies, two fine rings and several multicoloured bracelets.

Dressed as such, he went down to the *andron*, where Dionisodor was waiting, no less elegant, along with his young and distinguished wife, Theodula, and their two daughters. Women stayed there only to welcome Naso, then they retired to the *gynoecium*.

It was a rich *deipnon*,[88] and the two dinner guests sat down comfortably on the sofas around the table, to enjoy the food fit for a king – eels brought all the way from the Kopais lake that Pausanias had exulted in his writings for its fauna worthy of the most sophisticated taste, squid from

---

86 Room with a hot plunge bath in ancient times.
87 System of below-the-floor heating.
88 Evening meal for ancient Greeks.

the Euboea coast, mashed lentil, green and black olives in oil, endive salad and the usual *maza*,[89] all paired with a light wine from Chios.

After dinner, Dionisodor gave voice to the question he had had on the tip of his tongue from the moment he saw his friend walk through the door, some hours before.

'What's troubling you? You have returned unsettled from your trip. As much as I know Valens, and I know him well since it was I who put you in touch with him, he has a good energy. His presence lifts you up. What happened?'

'Nothing discomforting happened, if this is what you are thinking,' Ovidius answered, sipping some wine. 'Valens and his people treated us more than honourably. Except that...'

Naso hesitated. He had used his imagination, as the deserter had advised him, but it seemed that his mind had gone farther than it was prudent.

If he was hesitating to confess to Dionisodor the fruit of the thoughts at the front of his mind all the way back from Histria, it was not because he did not trust him. By no means! But he was aware that his mind had gone wild and was afraid he might put the merchant in harm's way, had he carried out his newly concocted plan. Nevertheless, someone had to know! And who else than a discrete, level-headed, worthy person like Dionisodor?

'Come what may,' decided Ovidius. 'I am telling you everything!'

'I can't wait, although I must confess that my suspicion sends chills down my spine...'

The poet scolded him gently, shaking his index finger and smiling.

'Hm! You have a brilliant mind, for which I appreciate you deeply. Thank gods you were not born in Rome,

---

89   Kneaded barley flour pie.

because this city never fails to sully even the brightest minds as well as the purest souls. And the ones it does not tarnish, it kills them.'

'Or sends them into exile, like they did to you.'

'My good Dionisodor, let us not generalize. I have nothing to repent for. Neither the cause I defended, not the manner in which I deemed fit to do it… I have supported the Republic, still doing it, have conspired against the emperor and I am trying, through my verses, to keep the Republican spirit alive in Rome, to pass information to the right people and do all these subtly enough to give the impression regrets are eating me away, so that I would numb the imperial vigilance and maybe, why not, somehow fetch the pardon. But while I have nothing to blame myself for, the other exiled ones are on a different boat. Look at Lepidus, called by the gods to join them, a long time ago. Now… I do not know which gods called him but I hope they offered him eternal accommodation away from the light… Haha! I can see the worry on your face! As you may rightly assume, I had a conversation with Valens…'

'Please, go on…'

'That man knows a kind of freedom only possessed by the beasts in the woods. A freedom with no limits, no restrictions other than the natural ones.'

'A freedom with restrictions, albeit natural, is not unlimited.'

'Well said. In the world we live in, we are free, but within the limits of some laws, some customs passed on to us in a certain way, that we have taken on as such, and, by doing so, we have laid out a freedom for ourselves, enough to live in peace with one another, especially that we are a species of predators. What we are doing to ourselves is close to animal taming. Those people have taken the liberty of creating their own laws, which are simple and have not become laws on account of being ancestral heritage. They were not so complacent as to adopt some customs, definitions, solutions or punishments solely because they were passed on to them under this name. The difference between us and them is that we are responsible for our limits and they are for their freedom, since the latter is the only thing that endures beyond limits! Within these confinements, we believe to have freedom just because we manage to survive. Those people are not gods. They are mortals and their freedom is contained by the time each gets to spend here. But we are free within some narrow borders and they – since they commonly hold in contempt everything that is urban, modern, regulated and narrow and because they are bound by a less than immaculate past only dissolved by the unboundedness of the starry sky under which they lead their lives – well, they are captive in infinity, which makes them truly free. Think about it, Dionisodor, Romans live there together with Scythians, Dacians, Greeks and whatever else they are. On this side of the city walls, where politics, aggression, deceit and mania all reign supreme, those people would whack each other unrepentantly especially if fomented. But not there! Useless to say that an agitator would not last among them not even long enough to think he might open his mouth…'

The merchant was looking at him with equal admiration and worry. There were no words left to say. The pause Ovidius took to wet his throat hit him harder than the argumentation itself. Nevertheless, he somehow managed to articulate something, and that something had reached his lips coming from his soul. Nothing rational, pure feelings.

'But… but… that way, I am going to lose you.'

… And Naso realized the depth of the wound he had caused his dear friend. Somewhere, behind his eyes, a scene was running, one he had not been part of – Tertius Valens killing the centurion. Except that unlike Valens, he had no intention to defect.

'My dear friend, you are not going to lose me. You can come visit me anytime. For a while, you might be followed, but after that...'

'It will be very hard to put your idea to use,' replied Dionisodor, thus proving his brain had snapped back. 'How are you going to...?'

'I will fake my own death. Damanais will be the witness of my departure, and the ones in Tomis will be looking at a cenotaph.[90]

'Do you trust the young Get?'

'Yes, he is faithful. Still unsullied by the humanity. I have watched him learning, behaving... I can vouch for him!'

'Are not you afraid that you will put him in harm's way?'

'No. I am leaving him clear instructions.'

'But Aelius Firmus is watching you like a hawk. I would not be surprised if he had some people paid to keep an eye on you here too, in Histria.'

'Aelius Firmus will not endanger his military career. Any complications about my death would compromise him. Believe me, he would be much happier to say that I simply expired instead of having to explain why there was no body, my own or someone else's in my grave. Even if, let's say, he knew the grave was empty he would rather show ignorance than risk being called to order. Moreover, I am going to shroud the location of my tomb in utter silence, counting on the fact that no one would take on the search for it as they are fully aware the find would only be a poisoned one. This is why I have to make the potential intruders believe that they are better off if they let me take my eternal rest in peace. Still thinking... Maybe some curse, like the ancient

---

90 Funeral monument built for a dead person who is buried in a different place or missing.

Egyptian kings... Or maybe... [His face lit.] This is it! A big secret, nobody will want to know since they would make themselves vulnerable if they knew it. And what can be more dangerous than the emperor's wrath? I was there, close to the incandescent core of power, felt its stench, know its secrets. Any of these secrets would start a real storm!'

'You are scaring me...'

'Yeah,' went on Ovidius, pensively. 'Something from behind the scenes of power in Rome... Something that... Absolutely! I have to involve Artemon and Diokles somehow. The first would eat me alive. I have been like a thorn in his side since I set foot on dry land. He is not fond of problems and I am, from his perspective, the biggest one possible. Diokles, on the other hand, is a nice man, but I cannot go over his head. I have to be sure that Romans are not the only ones to look the other way on this affair, and he is the city strategist... I guess neither Diokles nor Artemon would relish another term in the office but they will not decline it, if offered one next year. Ergo, it is a long-term plan with many variables. But you will see! I have everything in here–" he tapped his forehead lightly with a finger "–I just don't want you-know-who to move faster than me...'

'It could happen... Livia is weaving a web of plots around Octavius. And you are only a collateral victim.'

'Indeed! Do you think I am not aware of what I've written and sent to Rome? Even more importantly, to whom! Just that and I would not surprised if they dispatched someone to off me... But listen to me, good Dionisodor! Something interesting is coming up...'

Chapter 5

Seven hundred sixty-two –
seven hundred sixty-three – Katabasis[91]

I was not going to spend too much time in Ara Ubiorum. In knew the place well, but the problem was that the place knew me too, since *Undevigesima* had been camped here long enough. Since I had made the decision that my life was worth more than the military pay of a denarius[92] per day, it meant I had to also acknowledge my new condition – I could no longer be the brave soldier who had escaped by a hair's breadth from the Cherusci inferno, but a deserter who deserved to be punished in public.

I have tried not to make waves, slinking in the shadows of walls, hiding on the outskirts of the city among beggars, the sick, stray dogs, rats, cockroaches and worms. I needed to rest, both physically and mentally, and that world of the contagious filth seemed like a real paradise compared to what I had just lived through. Even in that place, there was only talk of Varus's legions disaster, but it was done in such terms that, if I called them 'exaggerated' or 'inappropriate,' that would be an understatement. I learnt that the Germanics were two-headed, four-armed fire-spitting monsters. Apparently, they did not ride horses but an unknown species of horrendous animals, with three-inch fangs and

---

91 Greek term, meaning 'retreat', 'a trip from inland down to the coast' and also 'a trip to the underworld,' antonym of 'anabasis'.
92 Mainstream Roman silver coin.

incandescent eyes. They were not born the same way as humans, but rather sprang up from stones, already of age, young and powerful. They would not grow old but when their time came, they did not die, instead they would retreat somewhere in the woods of the mystical, dark North, where they turned into ice statues.

But the portrait of the young Barbarian, despite the admiring terror it inspired, would not imply, by contrast, a dutiful pity to the poor Roman legionary, forced to fight against those dreadful colossi. Not even a bit! The Roman soldier was not depicted in very laudatory epithets. On fences and walls there turned up abhorrent graffiti, such as a huge phallus aimed at the bent posterior of a character who, I guess should have symbolized Varus, or an eagle, captured and plucked off by a behemoth with broken teeth and wearing a horned helmet.

I was grinding my teeth. I had set my mind on being as quiet as mouse, to avoid raising any suspicions, otherwise... Poor crazy people! It's so easy to sling mud! You were not there, with us!

The way in which the Teutoburg catastrophe was recounted on this side of Rhenus was revolting to me. What a pity that my righteous revolt would not keep me fed as well! While wandering through the Germanic forest, after the escape from Aliso, I fed myself with roots, mushrooms and wild fruit and it seems I was lucky to have picked the edible ones. One day, my black bird hunted a hare and saved a piece for me. Any other time, that ragged skull, with the eyes gouged out (she could not help it!) and half of the rib-cage with the fur soaked in blood and mud would have seemed really disgusting, but then I feasted on the leftovers of the cadaver as if it had been the tastiest steak, basted in wine and cooked on open hearth.

I had already been meandering through Ara Ubiorum

for two days and missing the woods by then. This is how hungry I was... Had tried to beg, but was not good at it... I could not run the risk going to who knows what places and offer to work for a plate of food, because someone might have recognized me. Even if they didn't, I would have been chased away, as my appearance did not present any guarantees. I could not forget I was a deserter! Right then, I realized that the skills gained during my military training could be used on the civilian streets as well. How did I have that epiphany? Simple. I beat a man for a crust of bread and I did it so badly that I left him in a puddle of blood and urine, just to be sure that it would take him some time until he came to and asked for help. Come to think of it, hunger should have made me only snatch the bread off his hand and possibly shove that prick. There was something else in me that made me hit with fists and legs... It was the war hammer that killed Furius, the spears that pierced Marcus Caelius, the axe that decapitated the lieutenant, the flames in Aliso... Of course, the beggar was not to blame for any of this. Or the people drawing abominations on the walls. But it did not matter! For me, that crust of bread was a win, but not a prize. Yet, a body left lifeless on the cobblestones equaled to a triumphal march before the Senate in Rome. I, along with all my dead comrades, strutting shoulder to shoulder, in a parade formation, through Forum Magnum, to the cheers of the crowd... This is an imagine that got stuck in my mind! Someone was unlucky enough to find themselves in the wrong place, at the wrong time, as we did, and suffer, one way or another, for the fault that the triumph scene could not be real. The first was the vagabond in Ara Ubiorum...

I knew that I had to go to Mediolanum and look for Servillia. I was aware of the fact that a long and tedious journey was ahead of me, but I was not afraid. My black bird was of the same opinion. She led me southward, following the course of the Rhenus to its springs. I was trying to stay away from the *castra*, even if they were safe places, especially since they all had received additional troops, after our defeat.

But 'safe' does not always mean the same thing... Not when you are a deserter. I was forced to run from Novaesium,[93] after yet another fight. The reason – hunger; the conjuncture – different. I had stolen some apples from a merchant with a stall outside the city walls in what seemed to be a pre-urban slum, full of shanties, a mixed crowd swarming the dirt pathways, while shady lechery was sold in filthy tents along with the most concrete bodily itches

I must have been followed, because right after I took off running and turned a few corners thinking I had lost my trail, three thugs showed up from nowhere and jumped me, even if the place was rather crowded. One of them got his jaw broken, a second one – by far the most adamant – tasted the blade of my *gladius* that left him with a deep wound from his shoulder to the elbow and the third one ran for his life. Things got worse for me when a few fishwives started screaming at the sight of blood. Several *vigiles*[94] turned up out of nowhere, so I no longer waited to see what would happen next.

After that incident, I began thinking of how to scratch up food and (why not?) money. I needed something that would keep the authorities at bay and the first thing to come to mind was to use my ability to swing the sword for the pleasure of the people.

The black bird took me to Mogontiacum and we both decided to stay there a bit longer, if only to try out the idea of turning myself into a street performer, with high odds

---

93 Ancient name of the current city of Neuss, Germany.
94 Troops in charge with the public order in the Roman Empire.

of success if done wisely. Mogontiacum offered the great
advantage of being an urban centre, far enough from Ara
Ubiorum. And it was quite large. I could lose myself easily
in it. The more populous quarters had clustered mainly
around military objectives, but my intent was to attract no
attention, despite the fact that I wanted to make a living
performing an act in which I used a weapon widely appreciated in the army. Any quick-witted legionary who might
have watched my 'performance', would have undoubtedly
had his questions. How to do my number, and do it discreetly to boot, that I did not know yet. But I was thinking
that, if things got complicated, I could have just vanished.
As long as the black bird was watching over me, nothing
bad could happen.

To be honest, I really did not want to stay there for too
long. It was late in the autumn and at that point I would
not have dared to cross the Alps before spring, but I still
wanted to get as close as possible to them and spend the
winter in Augusta Raurica,[95] which was over two hundred
miles away.

I started brandishing my sword in the little *vicus*
built around the garrison of the auxilia, in the south of
Mogontiacum. It seemed like a humble enough place to
practice my 'artistic' act before taking it to a fancier quarter.
And I have chosen well, because my success did not come
easily. The big gain was not necessarily moneywise, but to
have understood I had worried for nothing. Sometimes, I
would perform close to the walls of the military unit. As a
small community, it was rather difficult to avoid the soldiers
watching. Nevertheless, no legionary ever asked me where I
had learnt to handle the *gladius* so well. They were not even
suspicious that I had a *gladius*! That encouraged me. I had

---

95 Roman settlement located at circa twenty kilometres from the
current Basel (Switzerland).

rented a grimy room for a *sestertius*[96] per day near the stable of a rundown inn, owned by a shady Gal. With a 'lair' to lay my bones in and an honest way to make some money, I was venturing on the *via sepulcrum*[97] close to the Roman *castrum*, from where I could access the better off quarters of Mogontiacum. I was doing my act on the urban side, but more often than not I would look for a good spot in the market in front of the temple of Isis and Cybele. I just loved that place! The edifice had brightly coloured pillars, as I had seen in my childhood, an aerated and elegant hypostyle and the nave walls were painted with scenes from the story of the widowed goddess and the Great Mother of gods. The public statues adorning the entrance to the temple seemed to be watching over the market bustling with trading, heralds competing for giving the latest news, speeches being delivered, and there also room for the likes of me – jugglers, musicians, flame swallowers, actors and… me. Sometimes, whenever I found my corner taken, I would cross the bridge over the Rhenus and perform there, in the small quarter around the *castellum*.[98]

In a little over a month of my stay in Mogontiacum, I became quite a popular figure. I was making good money. I did not move out of my rented room, even though every day I had to walk through the graves flanking the *via sepulcrum*. In my life, I had seen too much death to be scared of that assorted army of Gals and Romans, buried in the same place. A silent alliance, only possible in the stillness of the eternal rest… The syncretism of the Isis and Cybele temple

---

96 Roman coin, subdivision of the denary, equivalent with four asses during the time of the story (the first decade of the 1st century AD), when a denary was valued at 16 asses.
97 Access road to link the vicus in the south of Mogontiacum (the current Weisenau) to the Roman *castrum*.
98 Roman fortification of a small size, mainly used as a watch tower.

was mirrored by the eclecticism of the cemetery. Just as the Egyptian and Phrygian goddesses could be worshipped together once they arrived in the empire, so could the Romans and Gals sleep side by side in the empire of forever. I preferred to stay at that inn, it was cheap. With the money I made, I bought some decent clothes and I could afford to live a frugal half decent life. I was actually eating two meals a day, even three sometimes that cost me altogether around seven-eight *asses*,[99] including a *sextarius*[100] of wine (not the best), while for a bath or a visit to the public latrine, I had to cough up another *quadrans*.[101] Had I not been mind and soul determined to go to Mediolanum, for Servillia, my stay in Mogontiacum might not have been a bad idea.

From time to time, certain owners of taverns, some of which were actually quite nice, were begging me to cross their threshold and perform there because 'auspicious times would follow,' they said. In one of the joints not far from the amphitheatre, my skill would be stirring rounds of applauses like nowhere else. The regulars were particularly appreciative, to the publican's joy. He was a veteran from Raetia with a big belly and loose purse strings, bright eyes and a ruddy nose like any good worshiper of Bacchus. When I was done with my performance, after cashing in and having my fill, I would mingle with the crowd. I did not bother to remember the names of my adorers, because I had no intention of making acquaintances in a city where I would not want to stay too long… furthermore, I was a small celebrity. And they were just glimpses – a rubicund face, another one scarred by chicken pox, a *palla* or a *camisia*[102] sometimes showing more than it would have been

---

99   Roman sub-divisionary coin.
100   Measurement unit equal to 0.5 litres.
101   A quarter of an ass.
102   Specific clothing elements in the Roman Empire.

respectful, which proved that those ladies were more than infatuated with me, a tattoo with the emblem of who knows what legion, a strange, colourful toga with its black hems, white midriff and red chest, a golden *armilla*[103] with Celtic patterns... Bits and pieces of life that stay embedded somewhere, in the corner of the eye and the bottom of the mind.

Towards the Ides of October, I left Mogontiacum. A few days in a row I had seen the bird fly in large circles on the leaden sky and I knew she was getting impatient. When I also heard her long and deep croak I quickly made my getaway with no preparations other than a discreet appropriation of a donkey, whose owner and landlord of the dump in which I had been a tenant, didn't seem to like him much, judging by the beatings given to the poor animal and the fact that he had caught on to its absence only when I was far away, on my way to the next destination. I made sure not to tell him where I was going from there.

After a week of riding, I entered Augusta Raurica on the most exasperating rain ever to have poured from the clouds. It had been pattering for two days incessantly, and those sinister jokes people called 'roads' had become almost impracticable. I had made my mind to keep going. It was already cold and the idea that winter was knocking at the door and the door could have given anytime, was making me step up. I couldn't say the same about my donkey for which my spurs clobbering his ribs were not a good enough reason to speed up. On the contrary. My actions seemed to sincerely vex him and, hence, he protested shamelessly. I started to believe that I had done his former master a favour by stealing him.

At that time, Augusta Raurica was a young city. It stood every chance of becoming an important centre – located at the crossroads of the ways connecting the

---

103 Bracelet (Latin).

north with the south, the east with the west, guarded by the Rhenus and a *castrum* where I knew there were two *alae*[104] *auxiliae*. Moreover, I was guessing that, after *Clades Variana*, Augustus would invest heavily in citadels on the Germanic *limes* and in those behind them, trying to fortify them and bring in more colonists. Back then though, it was quite a modest settlement, with mostly wooden constructions. There was a Forum, a temple and, most importantly for me, several taverns, one of which, located just behind the small theatre (of course, built of wood), had caught my eye. Something told me that, if I wanted to make good money out of my performance, then I had to do it there.

I found a little room for rent, somewhere, close to a mill, even though that meant a certain distance from my 'target'. But it was nice there, the host – a Celtic, who was a bit too much Romanized – proved hospitable and the small house was one of the few ones built of stone. This was somewhat reflected in the rent, yet since the rain was getting colder and colder, a sign that winter was no joke there, I told myself I deserved to pass the frigid months in human conditions. I had had my fair share of deprivation…

*

Slowly but surely, I made myself known in Augusta Raurica. I sometimes even had two performances a day, especially since winter, fallen upon on us overnight, was bringing people together around a mug of spiced wine, to the undisguised joy of the tavern owners who wanted to keep their clients under their roof as much as possible – therefore, the few city street performers, me included, were in very much demand. The spectators were like in Mogontiacum and (my

104 Roman cavalry units.

guess) everywhere: *tesserae*[105] unravelled from a mosaic hard to put back together again: There was the more generous guest, or the cheapskate, a more desirous matron, or the one equally oper for the asking but acting like a virtuous virgin, a scarred cheek, a *phalera* with Celtic patterns, a thick nape, a tricolour toga, with its black hems, white midriff and red chest, applauses… Applause!

From this perspective, winter promised to be peaceful. From other points of view, no! It had already started snowing, and it seemed it would not stop anytime soon. I had to walk in very deep snow to make my living, but it was anyhow much better than to have tried to brave the Alps. My black bird was nearby. I would feel and sometimes hear her, but she kept herself out of sight, for reasons only she knew.

Nonetheless, the months in Raurica were not short of incidents. One evening, after my performance, while eating alone at a table, a tipsy beast of a man came up to me and, without much ado, provoked me to a sword duel by telling me that since I was so skillful at swinging my *gladius*, I had better prove myself in a fair fight, not with cheap tricks. In reply, I told him that the fight could not be fair, since my mind was clear while his was addled by wine. I knew I could not avoid the challenge, as I had been provoked in a way that left no room for persuasion, but I was stalling and talking as politely as I could, as I needed my witnesses to see I had done everything in my power to spare the audacious man of any nuisance… At the same time, that would have saved me from any possible legal complications, had I killed him. It was not the case to push it too far though. Even if I had been lucky and no one had pestered me with questions, I did not forget I was a deserter…

---

105 Small multicoloured pieces, mostly of stone, square shaped, for the mosaics in the ancient times.

'Alright, smart ass,' conceded the provoker. 'Then, we will have to make sure the fight will be fair, right?'

The three thugs with him shouted their agreement drunkenly from their corner. They really wanted to see blood. The muscle bag laughed, looking at them meaningfully, then banging his fist on my table, made a grimace meaner than a death sentence, reinforced by a steely look.

'Then we will duel tomorrow, for all eyes to watch. Meet me in front of the Forum, right after noon.'

He turned around and walked out, along with his henchmen. The ones still there were looking at me with a mix of pity and curiosity. The publican came to me and advised me not to go, but he did not insist either when I refused him openly.

I was in an awkward predicament. Had I said no to the confrontation, the beast would have hunted me through the city, small enough as it was, and found me easily. Eventually, there would have been a fight anyway, but I would have lost all credibility and found myself in the situation of not being able to make money, which would have been at least undesirable. It was already winter and I had nowhere to go. I had to wait for spring in Raurica. More than that, the fight would have taken place in the corner of who knows which backstreet, at who knows what time in the night, not in daylight, which would have increased the chance of it being dirty. All four might have attacked me from all sides... Had I said yes, it would have put me in the crosshairs of the authorities. I was probably going to survive the duel. But the other one may have had friends and relatives in the city, who would have tried to revenge him. Plus, the Roman legate would have had to start an inquest and, all gods forbid, find out exactly what I was...

The next day, after noon, walking tall through the snow almost reaching my knees, I presented myself at the Forum entrance, before a large audience, where my eyes were caught by a tricolour toga, with its black hems, white mid-riff and red chest (a new fashion, perhaps). A few citizens, whose attitude indicated their good breeding, were going to be the official witnesses and had taken front seats, next to the entrance of the edifice. The man, who, I had found out, was called Adalfarus, was of Germanic birth and wanted a confrontation after simple rules – whoever lost his life lost the fight and the winner would not be accused of murder. Everything would be clean, and put into writing. One of the witnesses, tasked with taking down the contract details and checking the weapons, asked me several questions.

'Name?'

I hesitated.

'Corvus.'

'Is that all?'

'That's enough.'

'Do you agree with the confrontation?'

I shrugged my shoulders.

'Got no choice.'

Then, he turned to the audience.

'Citizens of Augusta Rauricorum, the man going by the name Adalfarus, son of Baldomar, has provoked the out-lander Corvus to a duel. The weapon of choice is the sword. Whoever stays alive is the winner. It has been noted that both fighters have understood the rules. Let the fight begin!'

Can you believe, my reader, that I was truly joyous that I had to face a Germanic? First, I had developed an obsession since the defeat in Teutoburg. Second, more importantly, the fact that the man was not a Roman (not even a citizen, otherwise they would have called him as such) spared me, in case of a victory, of too much trouble. For the rulers, there was one thing to kill a Roman citizen and another to send a Barbarian to the depths of the Tartar. Plus, the performance was free…

These thoughts relaxed me to some extent. I was therefore calm enough to examine my adversary. He was a colossus, like most of his people, with yellow hair and braided beard, half-opened eyes and the posture of a predator, with his head slightly bent forward between his broad shoulders. He was holding his long and heavy sword in one hand, which proved the strength of his arm. The fact that his two-edged sword was longer than mine did not impress me too much. Sometimes, the size of things matters less. What really matters is what you do with them. And you, my reader, with your perverted mind, immediately thought of the thing in your trousers, right? Well, I meant other things, such an empire, for example. Or an army.

Did it matter at all that we were the undefeated, numerous and extremely well-armed Roman army, when they massacred us in Teutoburg? It did not. So...

I found myself being chased. The man was moving in large circles around me. I was waiting. The first attack came with the cheers of the crowd. He swooped down on me and tried to slash me from head to toes. I could have stepped aside, but I chose to ward it off with my gladius, more to test the enemy's vigour. Yes! There was something there... I should not take it lightly. He continued to gyrate around me and, from time to time, to feign attacks. He was giving the impression that he was dominating the fight, playing a game of cats and dogs. Then he swooped again, accompanying his charge with a dreadful scream. A blow and another and another. But I was not standing in their way. I fended them every time, which seemed to disappoint him. Had one blow hit the target, the fight would have definitely ended. He stepped back, waiting for me to attack. But I was not going to do it. It worked for me that way. Seeing the heavy snow in which we were duelling and the cold weather, whoever was attacking too much would have exhausted themselves too soon. I smiled at him, thinking that it would anger him and he would charge at me again. I was right. Adalfarus was a strong fighter, but not exactly smart. He screamed once more and came at me, with the tip of the sword forward. The massive warriors normally put a large force in their blows, yet they have a big inertia. I knew that, he did not. I got out of the way and hit his right arm with my blade, from down upward. The blade plunged rather deeply and I had aimed a certain part. I had managed to section his triceps, which reduced the mobility of his arm. He pierced me with his look. He must have finally caught on that I was not a novice after all. He grabbed the handle with the other arm and threw a terrible grin at me, as if to tell me that he did not give a damn about that wound and could kill me anytime, even with his bare hands. But he did not dare to launch a decisive attack. For a while, he settled to do it moderately, just to get me tired or to figure out what blows I liked to fend and when I chose to step aside. Most of the times, I avoided the blows, because he was hitting so powerfully. On the other hand, though, I did not relish the thought of prolonging the confrontation. So, I started looking for his weaknesses. I already knew one, he was cumbersome. Another one, not hard to guess – his left hand was not as skilled as the right one in handling the sword. The weapon was making too large of a circle in the air, thus wasting time. And I waited for that circle, turned around and severed his arm, close to the elbow. The sword and the stump rolled in the snow, running it red, but I did not pause to admire my handiwork. I seized the moment of stupor when the Germanic was looking at his stump, still holding on the sword handle, flying away, and I plunged my blade under his breastplate, deep into his chest. He was looking at me puzzled, not knowing why blood was spilling through his lips. Death surprises some of us, as it had happened in Teutoburg. Take this death, Adalfarus, the son of Baldomar! That was for Lucius Caedicius, Marcus Caelius and the others!

I wiped my *gladius* off his fur jacket and left, to the cheers of the crowd, without parading it.

That night, I did not perform. I was not in the mood. But the next day I went to one of the taverns. I was a hero! I found out that the dead man had come from the west to spend the winter there and cross the Rhenus once it had thawed. His comrades I had met two nights before were his brothers. I had to expect revenge. I minded my business, had my show (even though the real mastery performance had already happened), took my money and left home.

I hadn't got too far when three shadows joined me and stepped in front of me at the first dark corner. To avoid the fight was out of the question, but the poor fellows did not suspect what would come either. Out of the darkness of the night there swooped down on one of them something like a winged demon that stuck its strong and sharp hook-like claws into the man's eyes, accompanying its attack with a low and long croak, as if coming from another world. The other two did not even have time to be amazed or scared too much.

My blows were almost invisibly fast. A few moments later, only two men were left at the fight scene, both on their knees, stupefied to witness each other's death – one of them with a slit throat and the other one with his chest cut open, while a third one was screaming from the top of his lungs while holding his face with stiff hands in a futile attempt to pick up the shreds of his cheeks and put the remains of his eyes back into the sockets. The snow was getting red…

While walking away from the massacre site, an image lit up like lightning behind my eyes; the imposing edifices in the Rome Forum were slowly raising, and I was not walking by myself on a snowy alley in Raurica, but strutting proudly, triumphantly, along with my comrades returned from the world of the shadows to parade together, shoulder to shoulder, to have our hearts lifted and then to rush through brothels to claim our trophies.

It only lasted for a short moment. Then the moon casted its deathly pallor in the snow and reminded me where I was.

Some explanations followed the next day, some remarks, while I tried to be as evasive as possible... Some people testified for me, insisting that I had really sought to avoid the bloodbath.

... The winter went by with no other adventures.

Of course I did not leave with the first snowdrops. It would have been silly to think that, just because Augusta Raurica was thawing, the same thing was happening on the peaks in the Alps. I waited until the *Nonae* of Junius, still expecting a difficult road ahead. The black bird gave me the signal and I looked into my donkey's eyes as if I wanted to tell him, 'Let us go together, there are some mountains we have to climb.' And he looked back at me, straight in my eyes, like he had nothing to tell me.

We set out south-east, passing through Turicum,[106], then in the region of the pre-alpine lakes and up to the Cunus Aureus Pass.[107] Despite the scorching sun and the blue sky, snow was there galore up at that altitude, with all the danger that comes with it. The weather did not soften even close to Lake Como. I only smelled the summer when I set my foot on the plain between Lambrus[108] and Ticinus,[109] finally to have a straight stretch to Mediolanum. The donkey had behaved well enough. As for the black bird, she was flying up there, very high, barely to be seen.

---

106   Ancient name for Zürich, Switzerland.
107   Splugen Pass, the Alps (alt. 2113m).
108   River in the north of Italy, tributary of Po river.
109   River in the north of Italy, tributary of Po river.

My heart was thumping in my chest, pulling my ribs like a convict desperately rattling his prison bars. Meeting Servillia was the only thing crossing my mind. What did she like now? Was she fine? Happy? Married?

I left the donkey tied up somewhere by a tavern close to one of the city gates as he would have me hindered me in the crowds. I rushed to the place of my childhood and teenage years. The periphery seemed stuck in time. I remembered places, smells...

But when I stepped on my street, I felt a lump in my throat. My father's old workroom was buried under weeds. I went closer, terrified. The branches of the wild oak in the garden were now part of the house. The walls were cracked, the roof had given. I pushed what looked like a gate and went in. My mouth was dry. The weeds had taken hold of the shed where my father used to keep his tools. I did not dare to shout. Servillia was obviously not there. But where? My vision went black. I sat down by the gnarled trunk of the tree and cried like a child, my face buried in my palms.

I have no idea how long I stayed there. But when I lifted my eyes, I saw the face of an old woman, deep wrinkles and thin, barely-there lips. She was looking at me as if she had seen a ghost. I was poking through my memories and found, in a corner I had almost forgotten about, the image of a flower lady in our quarter that might have been an echo from the past for this hag.

'Arrius?' she asked, in a weak voice.

I nodded 'yes' and she sighed.

'Poor Arrius... Everyone thought you had died up there, across the Rhenus...'

I found out that I had been declared dead. But my sister had been gone long before hearing this news. Even though, up to a moment, she sounded relatively happy in the epistles sent to me, her fate had not been kind with her at all.

After her mother's death, collectors started knocking on her door, more and more persistently. I knew some of them, my father would go to them for money to get by when the forging shop was not doing great. One of them, Rufus Melvius, still living and running shady affairs, was forcefully offering protection against his own goons whom he would send to torment honest people so that he could show up later, like a saviour, and ask for money from the poor naive to prevent future attacks. He was of course in cahoots with the rulers. He would send them the bribe so that he could be left in peace to carry out his villainies.

And Servillia had fallen victim to this crook. When she had nothing else to sell from the house, the only thing left was herself, and Melvius did not say no. For him, the life of others was just a commodity like everything else. The old lady whispered to me, while cautiously looking around, for fear some uninvited ears might hear her words, that the miscreant had sold her to a *lena*[110] calling herself 'Mama Gaia', who had happened to pass by with her retinue of hustlers and eunuchs on their way to Rome, where she had her own *lupanariura*,[111] in Suburra.[112]

I wished I had died by the sword of the Germanics in Teutoburg, to wander blind and naked through the world of shadows, to have Charon drop and drown me in the Styx. Any affliction would have been a blessing compared to the inferno the hag's words had thrown me in. But I had been left alive which meant the gods had a plan with me. The curse of the 'divine purpose' had followed me since birth, and the long croak of the black bird, heard at that precise moment, brought me somewhat closer to reality. In fact, it had plucked me from the marshland of the terrible

---

110 Madam (Latin).

111 Brothel (Latin).

112 Brothel district in the ancient Rome.

news I had just learnt and sent me to another roam, a world extracted from the common Mediolanum, an alternative Mediolanum, a world inhabited only by me, my *gladius* and an infinite desire to shed blood.

I got up wordlessly. I suppose my face was showing the darkness inside of me, so the old lady did not dare ask me what I was going to do next. Not hard to guess anyway.

With out-of-this-world calm, long strides and half-closed eyes, I let my legs carry me to Rufus Melvius' house. The two headsmen at the entrance fell under my sword, which seemed to have a mind of its own. I did not have to think of what I was doing, I just had to be there, to hold the *gladius*, as a messenger for a superior being. She was leading me, croaking her presence from time to time, gravely, as was her habit. I killed Melvius, then his wife. Their two children were next and when panic struck the abode and slaves and his goonies swarmed towards me, I killed them all. I went out through the front door, the same way I had gone in. Some *vigiles* had been put on guard, but the sight of a criminal soaked in blood that was not his, with the glistening crimson blade, was clear enough to keep them away. More than that, when the prying crowd understood what had happened and knew they had been liberated from the cruelty of that criminal, they started cheering. The crowd was parting in front of me, grateful hands stretching out but not daring to touch me, yet I did not see any of them. They were all a faceless gush. Had I truly been there, with my wits intact, I might have spotted a tricolour toga, with its black hems, white midriff and red chest. But I was not. Someone else was stepping in my sandals.

I only mounted my donkey and set off for Rome.

Chapter 6
Seven hundred sixty-eight – Two days before the *Kalendae*[113] of Aprilis

He thought his appointment in the college of *agonothetoi*[114] was a sinister joke, especially since their main duty for the running year was to organize the games in the memory of Augustus. Ironically, that had happened with Artemon's full assistance... In principle, he had been granted a great honour and, in doing so, the citizens of Tomis showed him their appreciation and that they had already welcomed him as one of their own. Hence the impossibility of declining. It would have seriously offended everyone around and, if in the past certain words had been overlooked, such behaviour would have been rather hard to condone. It was not about the money either, even if the patrons of the competitions had to shell out a lot of silver from their own pockets.

The simple fact that Octavian had not confiscated his wealth and he could still enjoy, albeit far from home, a nice income, should have appeased his rancour against the emperor who had ascended to the gods less than a year before. Yet his rancour was still there and all genuine! It was feeding from the muteness coming from Rome, throughout his exile, yet it went further back to the time the poet had enlisted the ranks of those opposing the ruler of the world.

---

113   In the Roman calendar, the first day of the month.
114   Referee, president and organizer of competitions in the Hellenistic and Roman times (Greek, plural).

After the victory at Philippi, the few supporters of the Republic who had escaped, who knows how, from the sword of the new triumvirates, had fallen into lethargy and pushed their beliefs and frustrations into the deepest folds of their souls, for the sake of saving their lives. The image of Cicero's severed head, placed in the Senate right on the spot where he had declaimed his speech against Antonius, had been more persuasive than the great orator himself had managed to in all his life. But Marcus Antonius's suicide, which paved the way to concentrating all the power in the hands of one man, had opened old wounds. The old and noble republicans had started, albeit still quietly, to dust off their memories and beliefs. Imprudent, entangled in the ropes of the higher circles of power in Rome and perhaps believing that the love of the Muses was enough to protect him against the brutality of politics, Ovidius had not shied from taunting the imperial couple more or less subtly in his verses, thus fighting his battles from the towers of the 'old world' fortress. He had no regrets. The relegation to Tomis had not changed his views. It would have been futile to take them back. He had written tearfully, it's true! He had done it to imply that everything had been a regrettable error. And that's true, too! But the recipients of his epistles and the people whose interests were served by the intelligence in those epistles were still his old fellow conspirators and protectors, no matter how politically engaged they had been or still were.

No! He couldn't care less about his rank or wealth. His beliefs were worth more than that. He detested that he had been coerced, by his election in the said council, to oversee the games dedicated to the memory of the man who, his entire life, had represented exactly what he, Publius Ovidius Naso, a knight and darling of the Muses, had deemed disastrous for Rome – the fall of the Republic, the rise to the highest ranks in the state of some bootlicking climbers, to the detriment of the aristocratic body, the imposition of a facade moral austerity, behind which lives, ranks, fortunes and cups of poison were gambled. And, not to forget, the persecution against Pitagora's followers...

To make matters worse, the gods had decided to set the Gets to the right of the river in motion, and the rumour went that their destination would be Troesmis[115]. The word was going around that Poppaeus Sabinus,[116] just reinstated as the commander of Moesia, had the army ready to strike. Not that it would have unnerved the Gets... The real complication, as far as Ovidius was concerned, came partly from the fact that if the Roman legions started marching in the area, that would spur the number of spies already swarming the Pontic cities. And since he made an excellent spying target, he found himself in the difficult position of tiptoeing between doing his duty as an *agonothetos* so as not to be reported on by the spies, and doing it with less devotion than necessary, thus not betraying his own ideals, in which case, reports with a different destination altogether would have lost him the sympathy and support of his old friends in Rome.

On the other hand, ample military manoeuvring against the Gets would have probably fomented their cousins in the city and in the surroundings. Moreover, he was thinking of the potentially dangerous situation in which Tertius Valens and his people could have found themselves, with the Roman legions fighting at Troesmis (if Troesmis was truly where the Gets wanted to get), a relatively short distance from the delta channels, where the renegades had their abode.

---

115   Ancient fortress, nowadays the town of Turcoaia, N-V of Dobrudja.

116   Gaius Poppaeus Sabinus (?–AD 35), general, politician, consul of Rome (AD 9), commander of Moesia (AD 15–35).

That old Artemon was involved in his appointment in the college of *agonothetoi*, was fully proven by his hyena grin upon hearing the news. That man's hypocrisy was almost divine! He made sure to trumpet everywhere that he wished to retire from public life because of his old age, but, at the same time, he sent his men to plant the seed here and there, among the market stalls, harbour stores, taverns and brothels, that no other son of the city had yet been found to be as capable, honourable and trustworthy as Artemon himself. And they had carried out their task in a hushed secrecy that not only starkly contrasted the old archon's loud and adamant platitudes in the agora, but it also proved to be highly effective. The fruit of their labour: when new elections came, no one dared to candidate against Artemon, since the plebes were utterly convinced that their city could not find a better leader than him, no matter how insulting this idea would have been to the intelligence of the Tomitans. With the sacrificial air of Prometeus with his liver being eaten out on the Elbrus Mountain, Artemon had accepted his reinstatement in the highest magistrature position. Then he had pulled strings so that Ovidius, the thorn in his side, be given a seemingly honourable post but which, in fact, had a lot of exposure and posed many risks, especially for someone like Naso, whose real status in Tomis and past exploits were widely known.

He had saluted the appointment of the poet with loud delight, and nauseatingly sweet words and history taught whoever was willing to listen, that the louder and in more adulatory terms Artemon spoke of someone, the harder he schemed in the society underbelly to destroy that person.

Diokles, too, had been given another term. He had done his duty diligently for twelve months, with no great feats of arms, but hey... That was the point! People were happy they had not been given the occasion to test the vigilance and skilfulness of the soldiers under his command. The last fairly serious Barbarian attack had happened almost two years before, when he was only a deputy and Crispus had been among the few victims. But the walls kept standing, the towers had proven their defensive use, while the moat had been worth every penny. Anyhow, the Gets' army coming across the Danubius had been constantly harassed on their way by either Romans or Odrysi so it had considerably weakened by the time they reached the city walls. The usual story... But the Barbarians had learnt from their mistakes... They would no longer venture that far out all the way to the seaside. Sites like Aegyssus, a few years back, or Troesmis now, as the rumour went, were becoming more appealing. They could be conquered more easily and were located closer to the places from where the Barbarians could get reinforcements against a possible Roman-Odrysi counterstrike.

At that point Ovidius made a mistake. In one of the epistles he had sent to Rome, hiding tactical intelligence behind his lamentations, he had complained that Tomis did not have the necessary military structure for an effective defence and aimed his criticism at precisely those defence elements that had thwarted the Gets' attack – the city walls, the moat and the towers. Not only had his words raised doubts about the truthfulness of the information provided by Ovidius among those in the capital of the world, but they had also managed to garner some frowns in Tomis. Well... As for patching up his relations with the people in Pontus, Naso returned to the urban Gets' good graces after he had read an original poem in their language. Across the sea though, it was a different story. It was hard to say how much of his confidence capital had been damaged!

One thing was certain – he had been appointed in a position he hated as much as a kick in the gut, but he had no choice. More than that, he had to put on a happy face, to keep the monster asleep.

Aelius Firmus was one of those people he had to act around, not necessarily out of fear that something might have reached the proconsul's ears, but rather out of his desire not to make him a worse enemy than he already was. The tribune came first to him to congratulate him – the ideal moment to serve the dish specially 'cooked' for him!

The idea Valens the deserter had planted in his mind the year before, stayed with him for a long time. That the poet was being tormented by thoughts other than the usual was obvious even for the young Damanais. There was a period, around the turn of the year, when Naso had stopped dictating his verses. He would let him read, assign some writing for the boy to maintain his skill, still trusted him with housework and provisions but no longer asked his help for dictations. In the boy's head, a war was raging. He was trying to figure out whether he had done something bad to stir the knight's wrath. Maybe he was not pleased with his calligraphy or how fast he was writing... Then, why would he not say it to his face? That was something he could do better... Why did he push him away? Zia had let it slip that Ovidius never stopped writing verses but instead of dictating them to the boy, he would write them in his own hand. He would stay up late and write... That would drive Damanais to despair! He felt tossed aside and, at one point, was on the verge of demanding an explanation but it was not the right thing to do! On the other hand, Ovidius seemed to be training him for something else altogether. He was talking more and more often about Tertius Valens's army, how nature had taught them things the city people had drifted away from, that those people were nice despite their past life and that if he was to die (and he would, eventually, this was the way of the world), then the boy could find help with them. He was not making any sense! On the one hand, he was sharing such private thoughts, on the other hand, he had removed him from the entire process of poetic creation!

Actually, Naso had chosen to write on his own, so as to protect the Get from the content of his texts. He knew that eventually the boy would find about it, but this could not happen before everything had been set in place, to the last detail, and what he had to do could no longer hurt the young man. After he was done with it, the dictation sessions restarted as suddenly as they had stopped.

'My sincere congratulations, citizen Naso!' the proconsul's emissary would tell him. 'Only a Roman could have been trusted with the responsibility of organizing the games in the memory of divine Augustus!'

He caught the sarcasm in the military's voce, but he welcomed the compliments as if they had been honest. He knew his political views. Octavian had supported the idea of 'the new people,' totally different from the 'old' ones, embodied by the adepts of the Republic, whose image, he had deftly succeeded in equating in the eyes of the people, to those who had killed Caesar.

Of humble birth, Aelius Firmus had climbed all the way up to the equestrian rank that allowed him to be a military tribune and made him equal to Naso. He was the epitome of the 'new man'. Rags-to-riches could be seen everywhere those days... The Gets even had a saying for that 'the head is bewildered its own bottom has reached its face'. All in all, the tribune did not have to hide his satisfaction at seeing someone from the other 'side', really hurt. But they were still in the agora and it would have looked bad to ridicule him, even if Naso, a master of words, could have levelled him to the ground, despite the situation.

'Thank you, my dear Firmus. I hope I can depend on you when the time for the festivities comes...'

'That would be my pleasure, knight Naso. But, I am afraid that my experience is limited to military affairs, which wouldn't be of so much help, I'm afraid. You, on the other hand, have known the highest circles in Rome and saw many things... Out of those many things, there might be some to help you with this work...'

'Hm! I have seen plenty, indeed... Maybe too many...'

The other one smiled, meaningfully.

'Quite insinuating... Subtle. Are all poets like that?'

Ovidius came close to him and took his arm.

'Let us walk a few steps, Firmus! I invite you to my place, to talk about seen and unseen things, useful or ruinous...'

The military looked at him with disbelief, but he accepted his invitation, from a mix of almost pathological curiosity and feigned courtesy.

They left the agora, taking one of the shady little streets leading to the harbour stores, and then they turned to the seafront where the house of the exiled one was, not far from the fish market, all the while chatting about boring trifles, yet each of them showing an exacerbated interest in all the platitudes heard or said. They walked, arm in arm, the poet wrapped in his toga and the officer in his uniform with all his rank insignia in full sight.

'Please, come into my humble abode, tribune Firmus!'

They walked in and Zia showed up, waiting for the orders that came quickly, in the Gets' language. Firmus also knew the language of the locals but he was visibly surprised how a Roman citizen 'abased' himself to using the barbarian language with the servants when – in his opinion (and not only his) – it would have made more sense for the servant to speak the master's language and the latter use it naturally and relaxed, as a sign of his superiority. That was another confirmation, if still necessary, that he and Naso could never fight for the same cause or share the same opinions...

Soon, the two was sitting comfortably in the *andron*, on the sofas, and between them, on a small table, there was a *krater*[117] filled with wine doubled with water, a platter with olives and goat cheese. The two toasted a *kantharos*[118] in honour of the magistrature received by Ovidius.

'You have very nice tableware, knight Naso,' the guest noticed.

'Thank you. The black pottery pieces come from Histria, done after an Attic model. My friend, Dionisodor, gifted them to me.'

'Aaa… Dionisodor… How is our good merchant doing?'

'No complaints. He is doing very well.'

'I know you visited him last year… And since then you have seen each other three or four times here, in Tomis – once with that ship coming from Crete, then the affair in Epirus and after that… with… hm… I forget… something with Olbia…'

Naso smiled and winked at his guest.

'The informants are watching, aren't they?'

'Then, let us toast to the informants!' Aelius Firmus replied in a happy voice and the two poured themselves another kantharos of wine.

You would have said they were best friends and Dionysus himself was urging them to rejoice, watching over their celebration from the beautiful drawings adorning the dishes – bright red or orange figures drawn against a glossy black background, in a symphony of proportions and hieratic gestures, vines, grape bunches, panthers, old satyrs and maenads…

After a while, probably lulled by the wine or convinced by the host's benevolent attitude that the invitation had been nothing but that and there had been no hidden intentions, despite the mysterious words to have preceded it, Firmus exclaimed:

---

117 A large and tall vessel, wide-mouthed, used to mix wine (Greek).
118 Two-handled drinking vessel, ancient times (Greek).

'My dear poet, I must confess that your verses, which I once heard recited in Capua, were music to my ears even though I did not fully grasp their meaning!'

'I am happy to hear that! Do you remember what they were about? Maybe I can clarify them for you...'

The other one frowned, pensively. He was making great efforts to remember them.

'Hmmm... I think something with... But no... The one with Aeneas is Vergilius,' right?'

'He is drunk!' Ovidius concluded quickly to himself.

'Yes, honourable Firmus, that is the great Vergilius...'

'Then, I don't know. But what I know is that I liked your verses. Very well written!'

Courteous, the host stood up, walking to the chest with the epistles yet to be sent and chose one of them.

'Please, my gentle Aelius Firmus... This is my latest poem. I have written it in the honour of divine Augustus and his successor, Tiberius. Do me the honour and be the first to read it!'

The soldier put down the kantharos and stood up, trying to stay on his feet. He took the roll from Ovidius's hand with a solemn gesture and opened it.

'Read it silently, good Aelius,' Naso urged him. 'Do not hurry!'

... His tone had lost any of its previous kindness. But the other one did not notice it. Instead, while he was reading, his eyes bulged and his jaw dropped. He had instantly sobered up and it hadn't been a pleasant recovery. For a second, he looked up at the author, over the edge of the roll, but Ovidius motioned him to continue. After finishing, he put the roll on the table, sat down on the sofa with a terrified face, filled up his *kantharos*, drank it up and then mustered the courage to speak.

'Do you realize that I could arrest you for that and confiscate your poem?'

His voice was wavering.

'Yes, you could, my dear Aelius Firmus. But this would only prove you know what is written here. As you have seen, they are not good things and there is substantial evidence to them too. Hard to dispute this bunch of accusations… Whoever knows of such a thing becomes an obstacle and we, the Romans, boast of a glorious past of overcoming obstacles, don't we?'

'I will swear to silence.'

'Admirable, but useless. Who would believe the pledges of a Roman, at a time when being born on the peninsula is synonymous with betraying? And who can vouch I have not already sent some copies to Rome? Picture this – I am far away and you are going to the proconsul and show him my text; by the time the information arrives at the Palatine Hill, it has already been circulating in the city underworld; they will then be looking for the source and of course they will find me, being already exiled. They are going to kill me… So what? Does it seem like I have anything else to lose? But you… Guess who will be the first suspect to have spread the rumour? Military tribune Aelius Firmus! The proconsul will testify to that, since he will only know what he knows from you. Unless the proconsul himself will be the one to point the finger at you. As you know, he is my friend. If I get killed, it is possible that he may want to keep the memory of an old friend clean… Because, for his part, he has friends in Rome and friends have each other's back, don't they? I will let you finish this thought…'

Aelius Firmus sprang to his feet and paced up and down the room, tensely.

'Why are you telling me all these?'

'It's simple. As of now, we share a terrible secret. Do not worry! I will not tell it to anyone. What is written here is not meant for everyone. I am aware of the cataclysm it would cause in Rome. Despite of what you believe about me, I too love my country. But as a poet, after a careful consideration, I have chosen the solution to be more … poetic. Can you believe that?'

'And what is this solution?'

'I will have these words graved on my tombstone.'

The other one was almost on the verge of an apoplexy attack.

'You, bastard! You will be dead, but I will still be in peril. I can be accused of conspiracy!'

Ovidius clapped happily. He seemed to be thoroughly relishing the scene.

'Quite insightful! But you must rest assured. This land, between Danubius and Pontus, despite its apparent monotony, is full of hideouts. My grave will be dug in a secret place. Still part of the… poetic solution. A challenge to the future. The mystery in which I surrounding my death, like an aura.'

'To hell with all these mysteries,' exploded Firmus. 'They are all bound to be solved, sooner or later. I cannot take this risk!'

'Wrong, my dear Aelius! Mysteries are to be lived, not solved. I am not creating mere fodder for gossip or speculations. The secret grave of a man like me, with a "will" hidden in it, becomes a "legend". If there were no more mysteries around, if everything was clear as daylight and we were left solely with certainties, then we would not need to imagine anything, as we would have nothing left to imagine; we would not set out in any quests as there would be nothing to search for; we would stop asking questions as there would be no more unknown answers. But does this imply a form of supreme wisdom? The pure truth? Or is it just a gangrene of the spirit or a mortification of the mind?

Or an easy excuse for a desired intellectual idleness, out of which progress is unlikely to come...'

'Eventually, the location of your grave will be found and your "great" mystery solved. Now or in two thousand years. Then, the conspirator's name, which is mine, will be covered in shame. The empire is too powerful. It will outlive this. I have no doubts about it.'

'Will it? What comes up must come down.'

'Nonsense! Look around you! We are almost out of enemies to fight against. Why do you think you are the only one entitled to worry about posterity? Why would I not have this right, too? I do care if people honour me, or not, after my death. Remember! We, as humans, will know all there is to know, at some point!'

Ovidius smiled. The discussion had slipped to place where he felt most comfortable. Despite his disdain for the tribune and everything he and people like him stood for, in the social, military and political context of the empire, he appreciated that the latter still had some arguments and that he hadn't panicked (much). He just loved this sort of provocation... Someone like Firmus, talking about posterity? Interesting how the 'new man' seems to take up naturally certain interests of the 'old man'... Maybe the old senators and republican noblemen should follow this trend and in a subtle and roundabout manner, try to imbue these parvenus with other most solid values too.

'All there is to know, but not everything!' the poet went on. 'Gods forbid, we ever get to know everything! Do you think this will catapult us to the top of the food chain? Will that make us immortal? No! It is going to kill us! In the absence of progress, extinction comes next. To always strive to push the knowledge limit further and further, again and again, this means to live!'

'Blasphemy! Are you saying that gods being omniscient

are also dead? Our traditional gods? The gods of Rome? What Oriental idiocies are these?'

'Ha-ha! No idiocies... As for the gods, they are not dead. They know everything because they are everything. It is the algorithm that includes the order and chaos alike, and I believe it would not be farfetched to consider the Pantheon not as a collection of individual gods, but as a unity, a multifaceted totality, where each facet stands for the attributes of one deity. Each god, and even more so such a totalizing entity, does not become anything in particular so as to be able to say at a certain point, "Here! I know everything now!" This is because such a god would become the infinite and the infinite is static. Were the infinite dynamic, it would be capable of becoming and having limits to move around, of growing or declining. Well, it does not have such a thing, since this is the very reason of it being infinite!'

The tribune covered his mouth with his hand, puzzled. He had been thrown in the ropes.

'What you are saying is awful!'

... But he came to his senses quickly.

'Enough with these ravings!' he snapped. 'And what do you want from me?'

'Good! Now you are starting to think pragmatically, like a good military man you are!' (Firmus' reaction was similar to waving a white flag.) 'Here is what I want... I will have to take some trips. I don't want any of your scouts breathing down my neck.'

'That can be done, but mind that not all scouts are mine.'

'I know. You watch yours and perhaps you might be able to divert the others' attention. I trust you with this. Think about it – the fewer people know where the grave is, the lower the chances are to have the inscription discovered. It that right?'

'Right. But what about the engraver? What are you going to do with him? Kill him? Buy his silence?'

'He-he! Neither. I will personally take care of his discretion. To make a long story short... are you with me or not?'

'Yes, I am with you,' said the officer, half-heartedly.

'It is perfect, then! Having said that, please, Aelius... It is late and I am tired. As early as tomorrow I will go take over my duty as an *agonothetos* and I have to be rested...'

Aelius walked towards the door, with the face of a beaten dog. But he did not leave! He had an idea! He was honestly hating himself for proposing a pact to Ovidius, but the circumstances demanded it. His rotten luck made him lay his eyes on that poisoned text and this was like an infectious disease – once you get it, there is nothing you can do! You have to look for a cure, no matter what... And his cure was an armistice with the poet.

'Here's the thing, Naso! I will propose an arrangement. It is clear that whoever reads something like that becomes an accomplice. I've had no knowledge of the deeds you have listed in there, but the arguments are solid and come from an insider. You have my support. I don't like it, but there is nothing I can do. As a soldier, I cannot allow something like this to become public, so if you take the secret to the grave with you and make sure that your burial place will remain a riddle for eternity, then... But I want something from you in return. So far, you have not offered me anything. I won't buy the story about the text being on its way to Rome. I know for sure you have not sent anything lately... And for the part with me being accused of different things... well... It is possible, yet flimsy. I cannot tell how much the proconsul is entangled in this, even though I am aware of your friendship. It is very likely the affair is still here, but I will not play down the risks. Under different circumstances, I would kill you to shut your mouth, but I cannot do it. As you already know, one of my duties and not only mine is to make sure that death will find you safe and sound. You have played dirty, which proves, if still necessary, that you are no stranger to such games, since you are here for a very good reason... You have put me in the middle of something I have never wished for. But since I have decided to play along and loosen the watch on you, at least I want to make sure that this will not be suspicious.'

'What do you mean?'

'Artemon and Diokles! They are well versed in the net of scouts woven around you. Were they to find out we have loosened it, I could get in trouble.'

'Artemon and Diokles? Ha-ha! Are you afraid of them? And I was thinking that Rome makes the rules here... That almost no enemies are left...'

'Citizen Naso, you know very well that a good master sends his dogs to watch his sheep, but a wise master also sends other dogs to watch his shepherd dogs. Or even worse! ... He selects them from among the sheep. My only request is for you to trap those two, as you did with me! In this way, they cannot say they did not know. At first, it seems to be in my best interest to have as few people as possible to know about this, but it is not true. I need them to watch my back.'

The tribune's desire matched his plans.

'I will do it gladly. Strange, isn't it?'

'What is strange?'

'This... you and I, on the same side of the barricade...'

The tribune thought it was a distasteful joke and so was the turn of the events. Nevertheless, he preferred to keep quiet and shake the poet's hand before leaving. At that moment, deep down, Aelius Firmus was damning the second he had agreed to be sent to Tomis...

'*Alea iacta est!*'[119] to quote Caesar... As for Ovidius, the

---

119 The die has been cast (Latin).

interest manifested in the grave where he was to spend his eternity did not entail his presence in it... But for the archon and the military man... Yes! He will play the same trick on them too, not necessarily for Firmus, but to gain some leverage against them as well.

Somewhere from the depths of his mind, the thought that he had just created an extremely powerful weapon emerged. Had he made public all the things he had written there, he could have spurred a rebellion against the system... But no! The poetic solution was ... more to his taste. Plus, he was too old and tired... And the cataclysm, if he decided to start it, might also trap people, either dear to him or just innocent, under the rubble of the empire.

Chapter 7
Seven hundred sixty-three
– Rome, seen from the mud

The wall of Servius Tullius[120] gave me the impression not necessarily of force, but of immeasurable pride. Approaching the eternal city, on via Salaria,[121] I could not help thinking of Hannibal, his epopee, of the fact that he succeeded in getting here and throwing the Roman citizens into the throes of despair only to abandon the siege. Even if you have only had a brush with history, it would be impossible for you not to conjure up the image of Hannibal once you have reached the walls of Rome.

Imagine, dear reader, that you are a citizen here and see that dreadful army that has hacked your brave and fierce legionaries with a steadiness worthy of any handbook of military strategy, coming towards you. Surely, you are telling yourself, 'It's done! It's over!'… You see Hannibal getting ready for the siege. And you know what that means: death or slavery. The shadow of a Roman army, the last line of defence in the face of disaster, comes out on the Field of Mars, their knees trembling, ready to receive the kiss of

---

120   King of Rome (578–534 BC) who, according to the legend, built the defence wall in Rome, still functional during the early years of the Empire.
121   A road running from Rome to the Adriatic Coast, after which it was making connection with other communication ways leading to the north of the Peninsula.

death, but at least to do it fighting. Then, something unfathomable happens – Hannibal abandons the siege, picks up and leaves. Why? He couldn't have been that impressed with a fortification (albeit strong!) after having passed the Alps with an army that also counted elephants! Could that army have been so affected by the defenders of the city? No! Not after you slaughtered the Roman legions in Ticinus, Trebia, near the Lake Trasimene, even with an exhausted army, decimated by the Alpine frost... Had I been Hannibal, in a previous life, I would have done the same. I would have turned around and left for Capua! I would have done that not because Servius Tullius's wall forewarns one, 'I am strong! Attack me and if you conquer me, the prize will be worth your struggle!' The wall actually says, 'Attack me! I will probably give, but the filth behind me will take revenge and engulf you completely, no matter who you are!' Yes! Had I been Hannibal, I would have accepted the dare of destiny and fought at Zama,[122] fully aware that my chances were much lower, but if I had been defeated, at least I would have kept my hands clean. There was a time when dying while standing, with your weapon in hand and your head held high and meeting the boatman on the other side like this was weighed more than earning a golden trophy, covered in mud and treason and paid for behind the thrones ... A time when posterity mattered, when you knew that what you did in this present life, would be judged in the next one.

But I was not Hannibal. And my 'Zama' was across the walls of Rome, in a brothel in Suburra. As for my judgment

---

122   Episode in the second Punic war (218–202 BC), when, after winning a series of important victories and reached into the Italic peninsula up to the vicinity of Rome, Hannibal stopped the siege and preferred to turn arms to Capua. Following this decision, the war was balanced and, in the end, Hannibal was defeated in the decisive battle in Zama.

after death, that was not on me, but on my black bird. I was just a tool…

It was ripe, coppery autumn when I walked through Porta Collina.[123] The city looked like an anthill. The rows of tombs flanking Via Salaria up to the entrance of the city indicated the only way in and out of Rome. They served another purpose too – they familiarized you with the stench. On the other side of the gate, the narrow lanes, lined with wooden houses, some with more than one storey, and others not, painted an olfactory picture rather than a visual one. They spoke of sweat, rotten or rotting flesh, faeces thrown out from the window by poor plebs who could not afford to pay for the use of the public latrine, the fetid mud flowing through the drain channels running along the roads, which were paved all right yet coated in gunk so naturally donned that you would have said if anything were to define Rome, that 'anything' was not the Forum, or Circus Maximus, but precisely that gunk. An undefined colour, combining all colours and none, an uncertain consistency that could have been anything from blood to urine, in a city that incorporated anyone – Latins, Gals, Greeks, Iberians, Dalmatians, Hebrews, Tracians, Numidians, Poenis, Egyptians, only to dissolve them and then coagulate them into a faceless mass…

May Hannibal be happy!

Well, it would be unfair to confine Rome to its slums. But it was not with my eyes that I was looking, but my soul which was only conjuring sad images, worn out as it was by time and chomped by the teeth of fate, just like the body housing it.

My first concern was to find a place to stay. I had heard that Suburra was a quarter of ill repute, but that did not scare me. I had to be there, close to Mama Gaia's pleasure

---

123 One of Rome gates, situated in the North side.

house, whenever that may be. I climbed Viminal[124] and then entered the valley along the Cispian[125] peak, through a place called 'Vicus Patricius'.[126] All the languages of the earth were there, rebelling against each other, in an indescribable chaos. Grubby stalls, with everything and nothing to sell, a place where barbers would shave your beard and who knows what else, for an Augustan *quadrans*, another shop where the only ones to venture feasting on the fish laid out for sale were some thriving flies; a bit farther a more affluent *villa*, at least judging by the two guards at the entrance, then the Temple of Diana, the only edifice where men were not allowed. Advancing from one 'attraction' to another, I arrived near an altar dedicated to Mercurius, located at a crossroads (where else?). A beggar told me that in front of me was Argiletum,[127] leading to the Forum, on my left there was Clivus Suburranus[128] and farther on, winding towards south, through shacks, there was Clivus Pullius.[129] The information should have cost me a coin, but instead it cost the bum a pain in his ribs, generated by the lightning-fast contact with my left foot.

That was the place I had to be in! It seemed to be close to everything. It was not hard to find a squalid room on the second floor of a questionable tenement whose ground floor reeked of cheap hooch and burnt weeds. The small room was a mould haven, with a barely-there bed, covered with a threadbare, dirty blanket and the ever-present piss pot near the window. The constant buzzing told me I was not alone

---

124 One of the seven hills in Rome.
125 One of the Esquiline hill peaks.
126 Road in the ancient Rome.
127 Road connecting the Forum Romanorum with Suburra.
128 Road in the ancient Rome, extension of Argiletum, running between the hills Oppan and Cispian, part of Esquilin.
129 Road in ancient Rome connecting Suburra to the area between Oppian and Fagutal.

while the smut scribbled on the walls gave me an indication of the previous occupants. And not only them...

'It doesn't bother you that the one before you died in here, does it? asked me the toothless old crone, my landlady. But he died happy... shagging a woman, Capra Cornelia ['capra' is 'goat' in Latin, n.tr]. They called her that because of her tits which looked like a goat udder. (She burst out in a wheezy laugh.) And while he was screwing her, Capra's husband stormed in and butchered him. Only him, he loved her too much.'

As I shrugged, not at all interested in Capra Cornelia's love affairs, the hag's verve faded away.

'I thought you wanted to know,' she mumbled, upset she hadn't found a partner in gossip in me, then she turned her back to me and left, hobbling.

To my unpleasant surprise, I found out that Rome was nothing like the cities where I had made a living with my skill of sword fighting. Here, people would not give a damn about it. If plebs were in the mood to see some sword fighting, then they would go to the arenas with gladiators, not gape about in the street corner. Plus, it was hard to find a place for my act without someone's guards grilling me with questions. Things were not going well. I had planned to take a few days to settle in and start making some money before going out in search for Servillia. But time passed without too much success, I could barely pay for my room and some scrapes of food. If I wanted to get in the brothel, I knew I had to show them some money upfront, so I changed my system. I still had some money set aside and I decided to take a risk. I was going to look for Mama Gaia's lupanar, get in and only get out if Servillia was running away with me. Where? How? No idea. The only thing I knew was if I kept doing what I had been doing I stood no chance of succeeding in my plans.

It was not hard to find the place. In Suburra, prostitutes were a common sight. Romans were always fond of expressing their social status with the help of clothing. You could spot a soldier walking in his uniform, from a mile away. The senator would be strutting his crimson strip. Toga was the cloth for a middle-class citizen, while his wife wore her *palla*,[130] more often than not pulled over her head like a hood, as a sign of respectability. On the other hand, prostitutes wore multicoloured togas, with many rattling bracelets, throwing glances full of promises in exchange for money. Their garb removed them from the ranks of the honourable citizens, but by their profession, they were loudly accessible.

Mama Gaia's whorehouse was on the other side of Portico Livia[131], in the northern side of Oppian spur[132], where Clivus Suburranus was going up on Cispius. The Temple of Juno Lucinae,[133] slender, with its exterior gallery lined by tall columns, was close by. Could it have been that some women selling their bodies desired to be in the vicinity of the goddess protector of childbirth or was this proximity a whim of fate?

A Nubian eunuch, tall, with a piercing look, welcomed me at the door. I explained to him that I wanted a woman from the north and he said that there was only one there, but I had to wait, as she was busy at that moment. He directed me to a narrow corridor, telling me to wait by the fifth door, on the right.

I slowly stepped through the patrons waiting for their turn in front of other doors. Some, more impatient, had already started pleasing themselves. On the grimy walls,

---

130   A mantle specific to the Roman women.
131   Portico built by Augustus in honour of his wife, Livia Drusilla.
132   Spur in the western side of Esquilin.
133   Temple dedicated to Juno, erected by Esquilin.

you could see the most imaginative profanities possible. There were scribbled there, images of exasperation, rape, the fruit of the wet dreams with distinguished women of the empire or brazen ideas on how the world came about. Everything on a backdrop of crushed cockroaches and human secretions, more or less dried up. A stink of sweat, flesh and burnt tallow hit you before you entered and, from behind the doors, you could hear moaning, giggling, farts, sometimes a slap followed either by laughing or screaming, in which case the eunuch at the gate would send some of his mates to check whether things had got out of control or they were just part of the game.

The fifth door on the right opened and a fat bald man walked out with a contented expression on his face, winking at me. I walked in.

It was her! Sitting with her back to me. First, she made a gesture as if she had wiped her mouth with the back of her palm, then she arranged her hair. She ran her fingers through her hair. She was naked, sitting on a shabby bed. When she turned around, her face got dead white and she hid it in her hands.

'I don't want you to see me like that! Please, go away!'

I sat next to her and took her in my arms. She was crying. We stayed there, I don't know for how long, without a word. Then, she felt better. She reached the ledge where she had a few bottles of greasepaint.

'Wait, at least let me…'

I did not. (Female coquetry, something I don't understand…) I took her hand, making her stop.

'No, Servillia. Please… That garbage stinks.'

I wanted to sound amusing. I probably seemed ridiculous, but she laughed through her sighs. She caressed my cheek.

'You know, I had to…'

'I know.'

'Because ..'

'I know that, too.'

'That scumbag Melvius was the one who...'

'Quiet! He was, indeed. He is not anymore. Neither him nor his family.'

I took her fragile palms in my hands and I looked straight into her eyes Exhaustion was written on all her face. A few wrinkles in her cheeks. I thought I saw some grey in her otherwise ebony hair. Her lips were a bit shrivelled. But behind the look in her eyes, I remembered the young girl ogling me, some time ago... O, gods! It felt like centuries had gone by!

I took her chin between my thumb and index.

'I've come to take you out of here, kid!'

She laughed bitterly.

'Empty dreams, Arrius. Mama Gaia is not a simple madam.'

'I am not a simple man, either.'

Fists were banging on the door and then a booming voice.

'Hey, what are you two doing in there? Fucking or telling stories?'

Instinctively, my hand went to my *gladius*, but Servillia stopped me.

'Everything is fine, Celsus!' she answered.

'People are waiting in line, retorted Celsus from the other side of the door, in a softer voice, but obviously angry that the work flow had slowed down in a rather disagreeable manner.

She took my head into her hands and kissed me. Her mouth did not taste the way I remembered. It was rather oily... a bit salty. . She helped me get my clothes off and laid on her back while placing my pelvis on top, between her legs, with disarming care. I felt her soft, overworked breasts quivering near my chest. When I got inside her warmth, she gave out a soft moan, probably the most sincere of all that had ever escaped her lips, which surely surprised her. She gave me a reassuring smile. I watched how a drop of sweat trickled down from my nose onto her forehead. Her breathing was precise and concrete, coming through her half open mouth, in the rhythm of my moves while her beautiful oval face was slowly leaning back, to match the pace. She was searching for my gaze and trying, every time she caught it, to tell me with no words that what she was living then was pure happiness. A grain of sand in an ocean of pain. I lost a tear. Actually, I did not lose it. It had dropped from my eye but Servillia touched me with her lips and got it back.

What we both had wanted in our youth was happening right there. But neither had imagined the path leading to the tender moments we had just shared. This is probably why we didn't manage to find joy in it. We stayed there for a long time, lying in each other's arms, with our eyes closed; yet, in the dark, it was not the prostitute and the deserter cuddling, but two earnest teens, curious and untainted, two young people sharing a beautiful feeling.

'I am going to take you out of here. You will see...'

I got up and started putting my clothes back on.

'I don't know how you intend to do it, but it will not be easy. We belong to Mama Gaia and she sends girls to the most prominent people in Rome. Don't let the squalid lupanar fool you. It brings a lot of money. Sometimes, we go to the gatherings of senators or rich people, even those with no title, as long as they are rich...'

'I am going to get you out of here.'

I walked out. In the hall, an old geezer with a shifty look and a moustached Gal were tapping impatiently.

The eunuch at the gate took charge of me.

'You are taking too long, citizen...'

'I want to talk to Mama Gaia,' I answered, looking into his eyes.

The man raised an eyebrow.

'Any complaints?'

'No, not at all.'

Mama Gaia looked as telluric as her name said. She was that kind of fat woman that the earth was pulling downwards, almost flattening her. She had a small and ugly head, with some white tuft on it and a flaccid double chin that was rolling down on the equally sad memory of some long dried up tits that, on their turn, were hanging on her rather consistent but equally loose paunch, the latter a pinnacle of dangling flesh reaching her knees. But the creature was wearing an immaculate, sleeveless *stolla*,[134] pinned over her shoulder with a golden fibula and sporting excessively red lips.

'What do you want, citizen?,' she croaked.

'You have a slave I want to buy. (It was only then that I realized I could not do that, but it did not matter. I had started the act and I had to keep it up until the end, no matter what that might have been.)

She looked up and down, with small and mean eyes.

'You don't look well off. Which one do you want?'

'The one from Mediolanum.'

'Aaa... Here is the thing, my friend... You cannot simply barge in here during my siesta, dressed like a bum and ask me, just like that, to sell you a girl. Do you have any idea what clients I have? I will make you an offer... Come here, fuck her how you like it, but give up hope I will ever sell her to you! That girl is going to last for another ten to twelve years and I want to make the most of them. After that, if there is anything left of her, or if you are still alive, we can talk. Until then, go away!'

---

134 Female garment in ancient Roman, a long gown.

As I would not budge, she yelled, 'Are you deaf or stupid? I said get out!'

The next moment, six eunuchs showed up, with their swords out. That did not impress me, but I preferred to avoid the fight, not to cause trouble for Servillia. They pushed me out to the loud guffaws of Mama Gaia.

I wandered on the streets, aimlessly, disgruntled, with my mind and soul empty, until evening came. I had failed. I knew that and it hurt me that I had promised something to Servillia and I could not keep my word.

I only remember being on a pontoon, by the river Tiber and my steps may have taken me outside the city because, when I looked around, the noise was softer, muffled, like coming from behind the walls. Yes! I was on the other side. Several torches were burning up high, telling me that there were guards in the defence towers.

I was alone. Or at least I thought so. My heart almost jumped out of my chest, with fear, when I heard the voice.

'You are sad, my friend, aren't you?'

The intent was for a calm, soothing, almost fatherly voice, but it nearly sent me into the arms of the boatman. I jumped on my feet, with the sword out. In front of me, a man dressed in a weird toga, with black hems, white midriff and red chest. You have to believe me, my reader, when I tell you that, since it was not so dark as not to recognize details, I can describe to you every drape, every fold, and every stain on the toga, yet nothing about the man's face. He probably did not have one or he had them all. Or probably, as he had them all in one, it was as if he had none. The hood of the toga, pulled over his head, was covering his face so well, that he looked like the origin of the dark itself.

'Who are you?'

For the first time in my life, I felt my *gladius* trembling in my hand. The man made a gesture of conciliation, as if he had capitulated.

'Right now, my friend, I think I am the one to feed you a bowl of warm soup. Of course, if you want to follow me.'

I hesitated. The stranger held out his hand to me. He made a hoarse sound, which I took as a laugh.

'Come on! Humans are not my meal for today...'

I followed him, somehow independent of my will. Was it hunger and the promise of a warm meal or... something else? One thing was certain, we walked a long way. I could not say how long. Or where to...

His house seemed to be near a thicket, obviously outside the walls. I had been walking there as if I had been enveloped in fog. I don't remember anything about that road. At one moment, I know I was sitting on a bench, next to him, in what looked like an inner court. In the middle, there was a cauldron. Despite the mystery shrouding the man and his abode, what was inside the pot was very earthy. The man had kept his word. He was cooking a warm soup. I saw him cleaning up some parsley roots and offered to help. He accepted and gave me a small knife. For a while, we both peeled the vegetables in silence. I was trying to see his face, but the toga hood over his head was hiding it very well. Oh, well...

He stood up and added the chopped parsley to the water boiling in the cauldron. Then, in followed the onions, the celery and the lint. With a long, wooden ladder, he started stirring the soup. Even if it was a simple meal, it smelled very nice. In his turn, the strange man breathed in the steam coming out, clearly pleased.

'It smells good, doesn't it?'

I nodded yes.

'Yeeess,' he said in delight, as if a magic potion was being cooked in that pot. 'Look!' (With his right index, he pointed at the steam going up.) The soup in its volatile state. The first sensation, when making acquaintance with a soup, is olfactory. The taste comes after.'

I was looking at him from aside, very carefully. I still could not figure out whether he was mad or the inventor of madness.

He took a bowl, filled it up and then he gave it to me, along with a wooden spoon, with its handle carved the shape of a swan.

'Go ahead and taste it!'

It was delicious, indeed. I slurped the soup in a few gulps, then I handed him the bowl, which he filled up again. The second helping shared the same fate. I burped loudly, as a sign of appreciation.

He sat next to me, again.

'Still,' I tried again, 'can you tell who you are?'

He seemed to take some time to formulate his answer.

'Let's say that… Let's say that I am an experienced cook. (Even though I could not see his face, I knew that those words accompanied by a smile.) I am the one to set to boil, in the time cauldron, people, facts, places… The steam rising from the soup pot is the soup in its volatile state while my cauldron sends up history in its volatile state, the history you are living right now in real time, the one you are breathing in.

My stillness was articulating precisely what I was thinking at the moment – nothing! But I realized that my saying nothing did not look good, so I started talking just to end that embarrassing silence.

'So, you meeting me…'

'The fact that I have met you,' he interrupted me, ,is like going in the garden to pick up an aromatic herb. You see, I only use fresh ingredients.'

'And what ingredient would I be, in your soup?'

(I succeeded in stirring that hoarse wheezing which stood for laughter in his case…)

'Hahaha. My soup… Well… I think you… you could be… Yes! I know! You could be the hemlock!'

'Hemlock?' I asked, amused. 'But the hemlock is poisonous.'

'Wrong, my friend! The hemlock is good against parasites. The hemlock lends wings to whoever needs to soar and ties rocks to the legs of those who have to crash down. Who and why that is needed, this is not for the hemlock to know. The plant is humble, true and efficient.

The last words I needed to hear! A witty reply, which could mean everything and nothing at the same time. I stood up and smoothed down my clothes, which did not look to good anyway.

'Well,' I started saying, 'I shouldn't impose any longer. Thank you for taking me in, for the soup and wise words, but I would like to leave now, if you don't mind.'

'I don't,' he said, mercifully, still sitting on the bench. 'But it is late and Rome is quite far away. You might want to spend the night here, though.'

I swear to you, my reader, that the next thing I remember is a ray of the autumn sunshine coming through the window in my filthy room in Suburra. Despite the great surprise I had when I woke up and realized where I was, I have to admit to have had a very restful sleep. I was fresh as the dew. I stretched myself but an ice chill went down my spine when I saw that the man in the tricolour toga was still there. Standing, leaning back on a wall and watching me. I flinched violently.

'Good morning,' he said, in a happy voice.

All of a sudden, that morning was no longer that good…

'We have work to do!' the stranger told me. ,If you want to stay alive in Suburra, you really have to know Suburra. Let's go!'

I got up to piddle, but I was sensing his eyes piercing the back of my head. I turned to him, without hiding my displeasure.

'A bit of privacy, please?'

'Alright, young lady… I will be waiting outside, but make sure you don't pour the piss pot on my head. That would be unpleasant…'

He walked out. A few minutes later, I was following him in what was to be an introductory walk.

We first went on Clivus Pullius, winding towards south. It was a narrow and crowded street, where you could easily lose your money, track and life.

'Suburra is a parallel Rome,' he started talking like a professional guide. ,You may have noticed that there are hardly any *vigiles* around here. It's easy to see why. Nevertheless, there are laws in Suburra, unbelievable as it may seem. And there are people to make sure others observe them. You probably saw some private guards over there. There, for example!' He pointed to a butcher's where a crowd had gathered and some citizens of authority were directing the throng to line up. 'There seems to be a queue for fresh meat. They sell mostly hens, ducks, pigeons but also rams and rabbits and more rarely, beef or pork. In the back rooms, they also slaughter those who owe money, but it is only the stray dogs and fish in Tiber that get to enjoy their meat. People are not here for meat only. If we got close, which we will not, for our own good, we would notice that clients are buying a certain quantity of meat but pay for more. For ten *librae*[135] they pay for twenty, with the difference being the protection tax and the privilege of being able to buy from here. Needless to say that, whoever abandons this privilege

---

135 Weight measurement unit in ancient Rome, equivalent with 12 ounces, or cca 327.45 grams. In this case, „ten librae' means around 3.3 kg.

or loses it, is dead meat. It is a prosperous affair. And that young man appears to be in command. You see him over there' He was talking about a smooth-faced adolescent, with an extraordinary skill in meat cutting. 'Actually, the brains behind the operation is his uncle, Iunius Marcus Saurianus, an old man living in that villa.' He pointed to a stone construction, a few houses farther up the hill. It was a two-story building with a fence looking more like a defense wall, reinforced with spurs. 'This is, my good friend, the area ruled by Saurianus's gang.'

We left from there. Around noon, we reached some places I was already familiar with and they were stirring up my soul. We were going up on Clivus Suburranus, along the Portico of Livia, towards Mama Gaia's lupanar. From the opposite way, a litter went past us. From inside, a stocky man with black hair slicked back, wearing a white toga, with no insignia showing his rank, was responding with bored gestures to the reverences of the passers-by. Sometimes, when he really liked a bow, he threw the humble man a coin and this person would pick it up, thanking his benefactor as if he had been given the gift of prophecy instead of an ordinary coin.

'That is Turdus Merula,'[136] my guide told me. 'A prominent man in this side of Suburra. Don't let yourself be fooled by appearances. His popularity has a price. The money you saw him throw to some people, well, the gesture is not random. Sometimes, this money returns to him, literally. Do you see those heavyset men in the shade, on the other footpath?'

'Yes.'

'They are his guards, helping with getting the money back. Now, if it happens that they take back more than

136 A pun. 'Turdus merula' is the contemporary scientific name for blackbird (English), with a reference to the black bird of the character Corvus.

Merula has handed out or even what has not been passed at all... Small details. They sometimes decide they want valuable information more than getting back the money, such as, for instance, the fact that a foreigner gave himself airs the other day and hit an innocent beggar who had helped him navigate through the maze of roads in Suburra. Talking about the guards... Merula's big dream is that his litter be preceded by six *lictors*, that is, he dreams of becoming a *praetor*. It does not matter which office... as long as it is a *praetor*'s! As you might suspect, he is not part of any noble family. Not even from the equestrian order. A few years ago, he tried to buy the hand in marriage of a young girl from the Fabii family, but to no avail. Consequently, to have his dream come true, he came to the conclusion that it was cheaper to buy the favours of some senators to intervene for him with Augustus. In the meantime, he minds his own affairs. The lupanar you visited yesterday – no need to ask yourself how I know that – is one of the many he administers, through Mama Gaia. His people also work outside the city walls. They kidnap slaves, whom they then force into prostitution not only in Rome but in other cities too. And when they set their sights on a brawny slave, sooner or later you will see him fighting in the arena for *Ludus Aemilius*,[137] the latter being in Merula's control, through the metal workers who have surrounded the school of gladiators in the Field of Mars, with their foundries.'

We came back to the crossroads with the shanty where I was renting my room. The man in the tricolour toga pointed to a chaotic agglomeration of houses going up to Viminal with seemingly no streets to untangle them. In fact, the place was an extremely dangerous maze of streets.

---

137 School of gladiators, whose existence is proved by written documents but whose location is unknown. It is believed to have been somewhere in the Field of Mars.

'We are not going to step in there and I advise you not to do that on your own either. It is the place between Suburra and Vicus Longus.[138] The only way you can control this quarter is to have the *cohortes urbanae*[139] raze it to the ground and then build something new. What I can tell you is that the place is full of altars dedicated to Fortuna, since the poor locals need her protection. What they do get is another type of protection, for which they have to pay. Over there, there is the band of titans, dreadful people who tattoo their skull bones on their faces and come out of the channels where they dwell. I will let you imagine the atrocities those people are capable of... Now, that you have been educated on how things work in Suburra, let me buy you a warm meal. I know a pretty good roadhouse, not far from here. They only have fresh meat, directly from the Saurians' butcheries.'

We went down the street towards the Forum and walked into that establishment.

'I have to admit to have been impressed with your performance in the North,' the man in the tricolour toga confessed, while we were sitting down.

I was still trying to show the least possible reaction to his words, since I had no idea how to react anyway. Obviously, I was nettled he knew so much about me, but I was covering it up. It was still unclear who he was and what he wanted from me.

'Please, let me order for you as well,' he suggested, in a friendly voice. 'I am a regular here...'

He saw the charming serving girl coming to us and he spoke to her in a tender voice.

'Darling, please bring us two portions of duck slow cooked

---

138 Street in the ancient Rome.
139 Enforcers in the ancient Rome, in charge with repression of the city riots.

in *defrutum*[140] and a goblet of *mulsum*[141] for each.' Then he turned to me. 'Believe me! It is a divine meal!' (It felt like we were old friends… Well… I could have played that role…) 'Indeed, the fight with the Germanic was truly special. But what really impressed me was the tempestuous battle at Mediolanum. Did you know people are still talking about it?'

'No…'

I answered him half-heartedly. I did not want to look surprised that he knew all that.

'Yes,' he went on. 'You are almost a legend… The soldier killed by Cheruscii in Teutoburg, has come back to avenge his sister…'

'But who could have…'

'Hmm, who else?! The old flower woman! She might have mumbled something about it, and whoever heard her and knew you were dead anyway, as they had declared you, saw the entire happening as something supernatural. You know what the rabble does… But Melvius deserved it. You may have gone too far with his wife and the little ones, but…'

I had lost my patience.

'And what do you want from me?'

'Don't get mad, no reason for that. I do appreciate the fact that you prefer an honest upfront conversation. Good… Here is what I want. Suburra is a place where the life balance depends on the stability among the bands.'

Our food came. The man in the tricolour toga wished me to enjoy my meal. I was famished, indeed! But I could not take my eyes off that darkness under his hood, where his face should have been and where the duck morsels (tasty!) were disappearing. I was gulping without looking at what was on my platter. At one moment, I looked around, hoping

---

140 Sweet, concentrated wine, used to prepare certain dishes.
141 Mead, a light alcoholic drink, made from fermentation of honey, mixed with water or wine.

to find a trace of bewilderment in one of the clients. My faceless man was not a sight you could have missed! But... nothing! Everyone was minding their business. They either found it natural or couldn't be bothered to care. Was it possible nothing looked strange about my companion? To the serving girl, at least... But, no! I felt my brain boiling. It crossed my mind that maybe I was alone and everything was a hallucination. I would have preferred madness!

'As I was saying,' he went on, and I knew he was speaking with his mouth full, 'the state of this quarter is a very volatile one... Ha! Ha! [The wheeze...] You may have noticed I like this word... "volatile". Well... when one of the bands aims to gain the upper hand, the unbalance is imminent and evident. In this case, it is very likely that Turdus Merula will become a *praetor*, hence he must be removed. The power vacuum will be shortly filled by his son who, fortunately, does not have any political ambitions. For now. No problem on this side! But if Merula snatched a public position, he would gain the ropes to expand his influence, to the disadvantage of others. Then, the Titans and Saurians will strike back and there will be a bloodbath. I will give you this–' He took out a rather heavy and temptingly jangly money purse from under the drapes of his toga and placed it on the table, to my right '–to carry out your mission. It is not as easy as what you have done before. You cannot go in the man's house, kill him and then walk out. That would generate turbulence, because his men would think one of his rivals had sent you. You can see where this is going. Instead, tomorrow you will go and have your little act in the square in front of the Temple of Juno. You will do the same the day after tomorrow and the next day. It does not matter how much money you get. What matters is to be seen by the right people. You will enter his service.'

'You mean that he is going to pay me to be his guard?'

'Yes... And something else – you have a few months on your hands. If the senators paid by him try to pressure the emperor, he will have an answer no sooner than Ianuarius, when the new offices are elected.'

We were done eating. I was looking, almost terrified, how the mead was vanishing into the darkness under the hood and I did not fathom, or refused to do so, what creature I was talking to.

'Let us go,' said he. 'Did you like it? Had enough?'

'Yes, thank you.'

He threw some coins on the table, we walked out and started going slowly to the centre of Suburra.

'What do you think about the pact so far?'

'Quite clear,' I admitted. 'But, after I get in his service, how am I going to kill him?'

'You will have to find his Achilles heel and use it.'

'There is one thing I don't understand. You are paying me to kill someone who, in his turn, will be paying me to guard him. Why do you think I will not betray you?'

He stopped.

'Because he will never be able to do this!'

He lifted his hand parallel to the ground and at that moment something happened that froze the blood in my veins and removed any doubt about the man in front of me – the black bird landed obediently on his arm and he caressed her affectionately. I could not react anymore.

'Well, my friend Corvus,' the stranger went on, 'let's have an agreement. You will work for me for seven years. When that time is over, you are free to take what you want from Rome and then go on with your life.'

The next day, I was in the square in front of the Temple of Juno, wielding my *gladius*, while the black bird was flying up high, watching my every move.

From the shade of the porticoes surrounding the square,

from the trees and who knows what other unknown shadows, more eyes were also watching me. I felt them staring at me while I was trying to outdo myself with the *gladius*, so the news about my skills reached the right people. Just as the man in the tricolour toga had anticipated, I didn't get a lot of money, neither on that day nor on the following two. But it did not matter. The money purse he had given me was going to pay for my room and food for a while...

What was supposed to happen, happened! At sunset, on the third day, the bearer of one of the pairs of eyes that had been watching me, a stocky man with a wide nape, came up to me and invited me to accompany him to his master's house, in a tone that was meant to be amiable but coming from someone most likely not used to pleasantries, it had sounded like a bark in a barrel. Nevertheless, I accepted the invitation.

Turdus Merula was living in clover. He had a two-story elegant villa, of a divine white. His female slaves were walking around, naked, as if they were floating. Considering the austere life standards imposed by Augustus, Merula's small domestic universe seemed from other times. The master was waiting for me, sitting in a *solium* chair with gold-plated arms. The roughneck who had brought me gestured to me to stay at a certain distance from the master's throne and he went closer to him, whispering something into his ear and pointing at me.

'You may approach me, good citizen!' Turdus Merula invited me, after the goon had passed his report, but he signalled me to stop after only three steps. What is your name?'

'Corvus...'

He smiled.

'You could say the gods themselves brought us together. I, Merula and you, Corvus... Both black birds...'

'Not all black birds are ravens and mockingbirds,'

I retorted and then regretted it, as I feared I might have sounded too aggressive.

But the other one did not seem to mind.

'But what other birds are there, my friend Corvus?'

I shrugged, giving up.

'Just black birds…'

His squinting eyes showed me he hadn't understood me… He probably thought I was weird. Yet, he chose to hide his thoughts behind a chuckle.

'My friend Ursus, here–' he pointed to the man who had brought me there '–told me you are very skilled.'

(It was my turn to smile, but only on the inside. Merula, Ursus and Corvus… You would think we were in a menagerie…)

I nodded yes.

'Can I ask where you learnt to use the sword?'

'Here and there…'

My hesitation struck him.

'Ah… Here is the thing, my feathered friend… I am always looking for talent. I need good men. The best! I am ready to heed Ursus's suggestion and hire you. But I would like a demonstration.'

'Here?'

'No. I have seen too many who know how to spin swords and even war hammers on their fingers… But there are only few who can do that against their match. Come!'

He stood up and gestured me to follow him. Ursus, along with other three goons, came with us. We went down some stairs… Plenty… Then we entered a warm and stinky corridor, lit by torches set in wrought iron holders, mounted on unfinished walls. A rats' paradise. They were coming out from all the cracks in the walls, freely scurrying among our feet, and my companions were religiously careful not to step on them. I could almost detect a dose of happiness in the rodents' squeaking. I caught myself thinking of the symbiosis between rats and people – some give diseases, others create the proper conditions to get sick. Actually, we are not that different...

We walked underneath Rome for some time, who knows how long... After a while, we heard some commotion which became clearer the closer we got to its source. At one point, much to my surprise, we entered a large, tall, circular room, with a fifteen foot[142] diameter arena in the centre of it. All around there were stands divided into three well-defined areas, each in the shape of a quadrant. It was reeking of sweat and piss. Lots of people there. A motley crowd... One of the sectors was taken up by people making up a dreadful sight. They looked like they were dead. I was told they were the fearsome Titans, who tattooed their faces to look like some fleshless skulls. The finest of the finest in Suburra, no doubt about it! In another sector, higher up (there were four rows in each quadrant), I recognized the young butcher from the Saurians' gang. Turdus Merula walked in to the cheers of the third section of the arena, and greeted the crowd with large gestures, as if he were Augustus himself. He went up to the most prominent place in the sector assigned to his clan. There, a beautiful dark-haired woman was waiting for him. She was made-up like an Egyptian queen, dressed in rather garish clothes and wearing too many golden jewels set with gems. Merula caressed her cheek with the back of his index finger, tracing the svelte shape of the neck, kissed her and sat next to her. I, along with Ursus and the rest of the goons, stayed in the aisle between the sections. In the arena, several slaves were raking the sand.

Turdus Merula stood up. The clamour in the arena died out gradually. First in his quadrant, then in the Saurians' and finally in the Titans'.

---

142 Approximately 22 m.

'My dear friends,' he started, stressing his syllables exaggeratedly, 'tonight, I would like to introduce to you an artist! He has not been in Rome for too long, but the skill he has demonstrated in his extraordinary performances on Suburra streets has caught my eye and this is why I am giving you... Cooorvuuus!'

Ursus pushed me forward and I stepped on sand of the arena, to the acclaims of the crows. Their welcome puzzled me. I was not known, had not done special things, and my introduction did nothing but irritate me.

Merula went on in the same vein.

'And because we want this artist to show us his skill in all its glory, I am bringing before you, to fight Corvus, none other than–' the right pause for suspense '–the Beeeeast!'

An 'Ooo' in admiration and fear was heard from among the spectators, which turned into a new wave of ovations when Merula gave free hand to betting. But when the 'Beeeeeast!' walked into the arena, everything went quiet as a tomb. Literally! Judging by the size and look of the one I was just about to fight against, the idea that the arena would turn into my tomb, with all its inherent silence, lost all its metaphorical quality! I was looking at a brute that could not have possibly come out of a woman's womb. Surely, he had come straight from the inferno! White skin, never touched by the sunlight, two heads taller than me (and I am not that short myself), small, black and perfectly round eyes, a crooked nose, as crooked as the mouth carved on his face, his arms almost as thick as a man's trunk, holding in each hand a gigantic two-blade axe... what else was left to say? The beast was everything a fighter would never ever want to face, if only for the reason that no fighter could ever conceive that such a monstrosity might exist! And when he yelled at me, what came out was not only that noise meant to stop your heart, but also a pestilential stench. The feral howling signalled the beginning of the fight and set off the bloodthirsty tribunes, which went wild.

The beast pounced onto me and hit the exact place where I had been a second before, with one of the axes. Needless to say he would have cleaved me had I stayed there or tried to fend off the blow. Compared to his weapons, my *gladius* looked like a toy, a kitchen knife used in a fight with catapults, Greek fire, Scorpios and other delicate things… I tried to lunge and stab him with the tip of my sword, but I realized it was futile and gave up. It was clear as daylight! I was about to die. Worse than that, I was going to die in the most disgraceful attempt to make it out alive from a fight where it was obvious nothing like that could have happened. After the second attack ended just like the first, it crossed my mind that it would have been more honest of me to I stand still and accept what the beast was bringing upon me. It would have ended fast, with just one blow. The good part was that after that I wouldn't be standing there to receive the second one anymore. The bad part was that a sincere desire to live only present right before one's death was telling me to keep fending despite the ridiculousness of the gesture. After a third failed attack, the abomination got really mad and let out another howl, making the entire room shake. I am sure that the people in the streets felt a slight earthquake at that point. He struck again, but this time, seeing I did not jump too far, he abandoned the axe when it had dropped and tried to whack (to sweep me!) with his bare hands. I rolled under his arm, despite the risk, until I reached the axe. I wanted to lift it up, but it was too heavy. I used both my hands, dropping my *gladius* and was barely able to budge the weapon; just enough to rotate it over the toes on his right foot and chop them off. A second of stupefaction followed. I did not linger to see what was next. I got my sword back and took position as far as possible, behind the Beast. He could not believe that those bloody things left lying in the sand when he moved his foot were his own toes. The spectators did not seem to understand what had happened there either. My only chance was to tire him out and wait for him to bleed to death. Indeed, this is how the hostilities were unfolding, after another two or three attacks. But even his tiny and smooth brain must have realized he was giving me an unexpected advantage by fighting that way. Consequently, he changed his repertoire of strikes. The axes were no longer simply crashing to the ground, hitting it, but rather they were sweeping horizontally, parallel to the sand. In that way I was also getting tired, as I really had to keep running. I was panting. I guess that the rattle coming from him echoed my panting. The people in the first row moved a bit higher, since the murderous windmill of the Beast's arms could have touched them and not necessarily in a good way. Then, I realized there was a certain rhythm in his blows. When he was attacking with his left arm, from right to left, his chest was left exposed for some short seconds, until the other arm was following the same direction. During such a moment of vulnerability, I jumped and thrust my *gladius* to the hilt in his neck and left it there, because I fell over the Beast's head, hitting hard the sand in the arena. I was praying to all the gods I knew (I think I might have invented some more at that moment) that my attack had reached its target and done it permanently. The arena went perfectly silent. The monster had his back to me and was not moving. I would not even dare to breathe. Then, he let one of the two axes drop. He turned around slowly, painfully slowly, yanked the sword from his neck, and blood gushed out of his body. He took a step towards me. I told myself 'That's it! This one is croaking and dragging me with him!' Luckily for me, I was half right. The first half! He did not get to take the second step, but he collapsed, breathing his last. I picked up my weapon and walked, tired, to the corridor we had come into the arena. After a few seconds of confusion, the tribunes went crazy. Turdus Merula came down from his seat, with a contented smile plastered on his face. He lifted my right arm, like the brave winner that I was. He was parading me. Behind the pride, in his eyes, you could read a warning for the others, 'This is my man. Fear him!'

When we arrived back, at his elegant villa, he ordered food for me. In the meantime, two slaves washed my feet and hands with rose-scented water.

'I like you, Corvus! You are a hell of a fighter. I want you to work for me.'

I said yes, while gulping some rabbit, served on a platter adorned with animal motifs. The slaves had also brought pigeons, fruit, wine and bread.

'I don't think I have to tell you that you will have to move into the rooms for my guards, but I guess you will not regret that greasy dump you are renting now.'

I mumbled something again with my mouth full, much to the delight of Ursus and his comrades.

'Tell me something, Corvus... I heard you stopped by Mama Gaia's whorehouse and there were some ructions... Since we are going to work together, I want to know whether my men are free or they are attached to some woman. Don't get the wrong idea... Love is a beautiful feeling, but I need men whose mind does not fly away... Secondly, I am not interested in the beautiful feelings of my men. Clear?'

I was all ears.

'So... Did you fall for one of Mama Gaia's girls? You can tell me that!'

I was hesitating. Finally, I plucked up my courage.

'It is not that I fell for...'

'Well...?'

(He raised one eyebrow.)

'It is about my sister…'

Turdus Merula looked at me, with his eyes wide open. Ursus and the others gave me the same look. Then, my new patron gave me an accomplice smile, while jokingly scratching behind his ear.

'Hm… My friend, you are fucking your own sister?'

I was bothered he was belittling my feelings to a sexual act defined in vulgar words but, probably because he had taken me by surprise or just because I was exhausted, all I could utter was the most stupid possible excuse.

'We are only half siblings, after our father.'

'Yeees! Much better!'

They burst out laughing so loudly that the villa rocked. I admit it was contagious and, despite the ridiculous situation, I laughed myself. Finally, after we were done, Merula drew the conclusion.

'Corvus, you are a strange man, but, as I said, I like you. Let us drink to that!'

And this is how I started working for one of the uncrowned triumvir in Suburra. I can honestly say that the short time I spent as his guard was relatively quiet. I was able to visit Servillia anytime I wanted. Her condition seemed not to have changed in any way, except that one of Merula's guards was one of her regulars. In a way, this situation was convenient to me considering that I was going to vanish in the thin air once my mission was over. If no one cared about my relationship with her now, I was hoping for the same when my new patron died. Not for a second did I doubt I would not succeed in killing him. It was just a matter of time to find his weakness. Anyway, everyone in his villa, except for him, knew that, once the man was gone, his son would let his father's guards go (in one way or another), for the simple reason he had his own.

The boy adopted by Merula was a royal scumbag. No one doubted that, once he inherited his father's empire, would take the old man's crimes to new heights. He had surrounded himself only with shady characters, as they say; it takes one to know one. His guards were not more ferocious looking than Ursus and his goons (me included), yet younger and more prone to violence. He thought we were too mellow, and quite often, when we were sent to collect who knows what money or to put in order the affairs of some subordinate, the princeling's clique would show up and, even if we were managing just fine on our own, we would find ourselves pushed aside, just so that they could instil even more terror in the poor citizens. I don't think Merula was told about his son's intemperance. Either he chose to look away or he took it as a sign that the boy would keep up the violence and terror, a sine qua non to maintain his influence in his side of Suburra. That the boy would give us the boot, there was no question about that... How? Well, this should have been in Ursus' thoughts, if he really valued his life. Unfortunately, Ursus was not really inclined to thinking.

Another evident aspect was that, once the kid assumed control of the Merulian empire was taken, the stripling would get rid of his father's mistress. Truth be told, despite her undisputed beauty, no one could bear the sight of her. Except for Turdus Merula, of course. Not even his guards. Or the slaves, for what it's worth. There was really something about her that turned your stomach. She was an upstart freed woman, giving herself the airs of an empress. Giving orders over Merula's head, harassing his people, much to her amusement; the worst thing, though, was that she had incurred the young man's hatred. I was told that once she had bluntly told the boy she intended to give Merula a child, who would be his blood and heir. Speaking of blood, at that point, it all rushed into the princeling's head who jumped to beat her. It was only his father's energetic intervention that avoided a killing. Merula was not stupid. He did not push his adoptive son away, even though his mistress had been pestering him to do it. She gave up, though, when she saw she would not find herself with child, despite their attempts. Turdus Merula knew some things about himself, as it was not accidental that he chose to adopt a child. Although he was rumoured to have been healthily hung and that he spared no slave, the truth still felt like a sentence- he was sterile. And I joke not when I say sentence, because this is exactly what allegedly happened when the woman found out. Had she claimed she was pregnant, it would have been obvious she was not carrying his baby. All these had taken place before I joined the group, but I was told that, during the respective discussion, when they threw the cards on the table, the hyena sneer on the son's face would have been enough to turn anyone into stone, worse than under Medusa's gaze. I heard that only Merula's threat that 'just like I adopted you, I can do it once again, so stop gloating!' managed to wipe that grimace off the young man's face and maintain a relative balance in the small universe in the Suburra villa. But the hostility between the lad and woman stayed intact.

That's how things were in my patron's house. Outside of it, we were minding our own affairs, trying not to step on the toes of our rivals. And so did they.

From Curia,[143] though, the news was not what we expected. Even if he had been slipping backhanders to senators, they seemed to have failed to persuade the emperor to select Merula's name for the electoral lists. The fact that he was not part of an old family lineage was not necessarily an obstacle. Augustus was supporting new people.

---

143 The Roman senate.

Nevertheless, Augustus was not out of touch with the masses, and, whatever was happening in Suburra, it did not mean that he was not aware of it, only that he tolerated it, so as not to cause a stir right in the heart of Rome, behind the Forum. He was probably waiting for the right time to step in and sweep up the place.

My patron was not a man that would give up that easily. He bribed some more, reached out to other heavyweights from among the senators, all for those six lictors, with everything pertaining to their presence. His obstinacy to get a taste of power did not let me forget what I was actually doing there and rightfully so!

I remembered me being the hemlock, at least for the man in the tricolour toga, and it seemed funny to use precisely this thing. It was not difficult to score some powder of hemlock seeds. I knew the wine was the remedy but, paradoxically, seeds were fatal if ingested with wine.

I felt sorry for Merula. The time I had served him was not that bad, but it was time to end his days. A bit of powder in a *pocula* of wine, at a moment I was sure he would drink only with his woman so that there was a scapegoat, and the rest is easy to guess. Everyone was pointing to her. Alerted by screams, we stormed into the room, saw the spots on the patron's body, specific to poisoning with hemlock, as well as his death, and exchanged a look among ourselves, silently agreeing that the only suspect was the loathsome mistress, so we trialled her that way and proceed to killing her and throwing her body in Cloaca Maxima.[144] By the time her body would have emerged in the Tiber, it would be barely recognizable. If it ever did! As for us, things were quite clear, once the princeling rose to power – we flicked out of sight, every which way. Ursus killed himself. He did not know any better...

---

144 Part of the sewage system in ancient Rome

I had to disappear from Rome and it was killing me that I could no longer see Servillia. However, the man in the tricolour toga assured me there was still hope. First, he guaranteed her safety. Second, he was going to take me out of the world capital, at least for a while. But, third, I was still under his contract, which meant he had more work for me and I would come back to the city anytime it was necessary. Until then, my new abode was going to be Sulmo,[145] a small and lovely town ninety miles away from The Eternal City.

---

145 Ancient name of Sulmona

Chapter 8
Seven hundred sixty-nine
– Around *Nonae*[146] of Maius

Histria was a delight at that time of the year. The old city, which, according to tradition, was founded during the thirty third Olympiad,[147] had not lost one bit of its grace and prestige of yore. It was vibrant. Especially during spring, when the breeze was cool, the city would fill with a pleasant sea whiff, not at all pungent, and people seemed to have borrowed something from the raw green of the leaves in the trees. Histria was a green city, thanks to the large number of elegant villas, surrounded by their gardens. Its large square, with a chain of temples, was bustling with the throng of merchants yelling at the top of their lungs words to sell their wares, only different in price, since they were coming from just a few sources, one of them being prosperous Dionisodor. But that did not stop them from touting their goods as if nothing like them.

It had been a troubled time, with the Gets conquering Troesmis and, thus, blocking the movement of wares to and from the North, across Istros, then the Moesia legions stepping in forcefully, to liberate the city. Nevertheless, Histria

---

146 In the Roman calendar, the seventh day of the months Martius, Maius, Iulius and October, but the fifth for the others; in this case, 'around Nonae of Maius' means 'between 2 and 7 of May', since the first day has the distinct name of Kalendae.
147 Circa 657 BC.

seemed well above all this. It was a strong city in every way and the barbarian attack, even if it had been aimed at an important city, at a relatively short distance, compared to the magnitude of the trading connections of Histria, it did not succeed in causing consequences so big as to affect the city economy. Incidentally, had the Gets been able to maintain control over Troesmis and even to attack Ibida,[148] as planned, *that* would have meant great trouble indeed...

At that beginning of Maius, Dionisodor gladly welcomed a new visit by his Roman friend from Tomis. An epistle sent a few days before by Ovidius had let the merchant know about his travel intentions and since the reply had been affirmative (how else?), the meeting was a sure thing.

'My dear Naso!' Dionisodor greeted him with open arms, after his slaves had put down the packs of the Roman and of his young disciple.

'You are always radiant, Dionisodor! I am so happy you have agreed to my visit.'

Ovidius took his *petasus*[149]off his head and the two embraced, like the good friends they were.

'How can I deny myself of your bright presence?' replied the merchant. 'Please, come in. I believe you are tired... Let Damanais go straight to the kitchen and you do me the honour of following me.'

'Gladly! I have to admit that the journey was not that difficult. We joined a caravan coming from Callatis[150] and... here we are!'

They had reached the interior garden of Dionisodor's house. The artesian well was sprinkling a blessed coolness,

---

148 Ancient fortress, located in the area of current village Slava Rusă, Tulcea county.
149 A broad-brimmed hat, usually for travelling, in ancient times (Latin).
150 Greek colony, the current city of Mangalia.

while the laurel shrubs planted in large pots, around the water, were spreading a delicate scent. The host and his guest sat on a bench, in the shade of the colonnade overlooking the garden, while a slave brought them a pocula with cold water and lemon.

'Apart from my desire to see you again,' said Ovidius, after wetting his lips with the drink, my visit has also another intertion...'

'Whatever that is,' Dionisodor interrupted him, 'you will tell me tomorrow morning, during *akratismos*.[151] As I understood from your epistle, you will be here for a few days, so there is no need to hasten. I am sure the intention will be fulfilled. Until then, my dear, I invite you to have a rest. I have prepared a *symposion*[152] tonight in your honour, and I invited a few outstanding people in Histria. Some of them, you already krow...'

As Dionisodor had promised, the banquet in honour of the guest from Tomis was going to be graced by the presence of the 'gentry' in the city – the great priest of Apollo, a respectable old man of a few words, yet agile in gestures, about whom legend said to have been descended from the old lineage of Argadei,[153] the commander of the guards, members of the *boule*[154], poets, some of them admirers of Ovidius's verses, vessel proprietors and several fellow affluent merchants. To start with, they served cookies with honey, pecans and pearuts, after which, before indulging in wine, music and games, Dionisodor poured the libation. Naso had the honour to raise an ode to Dionysus and the Tomis poet recited from Homer, the timeless bard. Singers and acrobats, jugglers and dancers have graced the wonderful

---

151 Breakfast (Greek).
152 Banquet (Greek).
153 One of the six Miletus city founders' tribes.
154 Council, as a governing body in ancient Greece.

evening that would not have been perfect had a 'king of the banquet' not been chosen, in the person (surprise!) of Damanais. Despite his modest origin, he had succeeded in charming everyone with his Greek and Latin and unexpected erudition in philosophy and history. His master was looking with genuine pride at the way he was acclaimed for his confident and correct answers during the game of questions which the younger guests were playing.

After a short, yet deep sleep, the first light of the day found the merchant and his notable guest around a light breakfast, with *akratos*[155] soaked in white wine and *tagenites*[156] with honey and sour milk.

'It was an unforgettable evening, Dionisodor. I am grateful, even though I am not certain I am worth this honour...'

'Don't be so humble, Naso. You know you deserve much more. We are not talking about a banquet here, or any office you will have received in Tomis... Or even the tax break you are enjoying now... [The two shared a bitter laugh.] But we are talking about you. You are neither the poet of Rome, nor of Tomis. You are the poet of the entire world and only a cruel fate threw you on this land. Don't misunderstand me... I am glad it is here, otherwise I would be poorer, despite the gold I have. My life would be miserable. But what is the meaning of my life? Who am I? Who will remember me after I die? But you are who you are and will continue to live, through your verses, after your body turns to dust.'

'Your words comfort me, my friend. You have something that makes my exile more bearable and I have to confess that, for my part, I could not have considered myself an accomplished man, had I not met you. See how the gods have taken good care of us? It was needed an exile to fill two hearts up.'

---

155 Barley bread (Greek).
156 Pie made from wheat flour, with olive oil (Greek).

'Fate…'

'True. I was saying yesterday that my visit had an intention. Well, this intention is to tempt fate.'

Dionisodor raised himself up on one elbow on his *kliné*,[157] looking worriedly at his friend: 'What you are saying scares me. I was hoping you would be freed of those thoughts…'

'I have not, Dionisodor… haven't managed to… Searching for freedom is part of human nature. I do not want to break the imperial decree. That would bring disrepute to me before prompting my end. I accepted the situation, but that does not mean I cannot wish to trade the bars within me for that infinite prison Valens was telling me about…'

'I understand and I can promise you that, despite the sadness this affair inflicts on me, I will no longer doubt your reasoning or try to make you abandon it. So… How I can be of help?'

'I need a sculptor to engrave an inscription in Latin. It must be one who does not have an earthly idea of what he is writing. I could have found someone like that in Tomis, but there are too many eyes and ears over there. I am sure the same is here. But, to have my plan work, I have used a small ruse on Aelius Firmus, Artemon and Diokles. I have reasons to believe that they have taken the bait, and that, here at least, in Histria, I am less vulnerable than there.'

'I know exactly the man you need, but please, will you at least tell me, if you can, what is so unusual about the text of the inscription that you don't want the sculptor to understand it?'

'Dionisodor, you are my friend. This is why I will not reveal the content to you. It is for your own and your family's good. I am trying to protect you and, for this reason, I am pleading with you not to try to find out.'

---

157 Sofa (Greek)

The merchant nodded his head, sombrely. There are things in this world to give the measure of loyalty and appreciation more than a thousand words. They are called 'codes of silence' and hold unsaid justifications. Such silence, like an oath of allegiance, settled between them.

A few hours later, they found themselves in front of sculptor Nicanor's atelier. He was an old stonemason who had served his apprenticeship during his faraway younger days with famous masters in Greece at their own places. He had declined learning Latin, as he was one of those proud Greeks for whom civilization started and ended at the Aegean Sea. The fact that the world had now new rulers was just an administrative detail...

North and south of Pontus Euxinus, his atelier sent statues of gods in immaculate marble or bronze, no different than the immortal works of Praxiteles of Athens or Anaxagoras of Aegina, the one gifted by Zeus in Olympia himself. The stewards of the best-known temples on the west shore of the Pontus Euxinus were commissioning altars and columns, and his fame had long crossed the Bosporus.

It was not the first time that he had been asked to work with a text in Latin. There were usually people, like Ovidius, who wanted to ensure that whatever had to be written was meant to remain a secret (the operative word being 'remain'). Nicanor never asked why. He could have asked someone speaking Latin to translate the foreign letters he was engraving in stone. But he would not do it. He had never done it! He was a man of honour! And that honour came with a price.

'Seven drachmas a day, multiplied by three days' work!'

Like a good merchant he was, Dionisodor started haggling.

'Seven drachmas! It's exorbitant! Not even in Athens would you hear that price, for a simple inscription!'

145

The sculptor shrugged his shoulders, wiped his hands on his apron made of tanned, white, lamb skin and turned to one of his apprentices, seemingly to instruct him in whatever he was doing, but actually faking disinterest and letting the clients understand the discussion had finished.

'Four drachmas,' suggested Dionisodor, in a tone of concession, but he did not succeed in stirring any reaction from the master.

Thinking (in horror!) that the negotiation could have ended before starting, the merchant bargained over his own price.

'Four drachmas and two *diobols*![158] It's a good offer...'

Not a sign! The sculptor's full attention seemed to have been turned to his apprentice. Then, Ovidius spoke.

'Master Nicanor, please tell me what is included in the price of seven obols you are asking?'

It is only then, the stone master heeded them again.

'My full discretion.'

'Good,' the poet assented, to the merchant's visible dissatisfaction. 'Instead of tangling in numbers or lamenting for not having haggled, I will give you ten *staters*[159] for the three days of work; when it is done, you seal the inscription in wax and put it under lock, in a wooden reliquary. My friend Dionisodor, here present, will come to fetch it from you.'

Nicanor clasped hands with Ovidius, not forgetting to show an air of superiority, especially now when saying goodbye to the merchant. There were not too many in Histria to brag about a victory against Dionisodor...

---

158 Subdivision of drachma, in ancient Greek, equivalent to 2 obols. An obol means 1/6 of a drachma. In this case, 'two diobols' means 4/6 of a drachma.

159 Stater is a monetary unit, equivalent with two drachmas, in ancient times. Better known name was 'didrachma'. In this case, 'ten staters' means twenty drachmas.

'I had him wrapped him around my little finger,' he mumbled while they were leaving. 'I could have paid him three gallons of olive oil…'

Same day, after noon, Ovidius and Damanais, along with other three of the merchant's trusted men, given by him as escort, set off for the mouth of Danubius. They had to ride more than five hundred stades[160] to the small village of Valens.

They arrived there at dusk. The escort was ordered to spend the night there and go back to Histria at dawn.

'What winds bring you here, my good Naso?,' the deserter welcomed him.

'Fair winds, as they say,' answered the poet while dismounting. 'I am here to find freedom.'

Tertius Valens looked at him from the side, smiling amusedly.

'Then, you are in the right place.'

He put his hand around his shoulder and both of them walked in the hut of the former *tesserarius*. What they talked in there, well into the night, it is only for them to know. What is certain is that, the next day, after Dionisodor's people had left, Tertius Valens told his comrades he would also leave together with the poet, Gnur and Septimius Macer, while Damanais was to stay behind in the care of the rest of the tribe, until they returned.

'Where to?' asked the disciple.

'You will find out, my child,' answered Naso, caressing his head. 'But not now. When the right time comes.'

The Scythian saw to it personally to fill up the goatskin bottles with fresh water and pack the grub for the journey, while Macer was saddling up the horses. When they finished the preparations, all four set out on their way and

---

160 Measurement unit for length, equivalent to circa 158 m. In this case, 'five hundred of stades' is equal to 79 km.

came back the next day, after sunset. They looked like they had found what they had searched for.

As if they knew when the travellers were about to come back, Valens's people welcomed them with a campfire burning and a ram, roasting in a cooking pit. Another night to remember followed, with gaiety, wine and bawdy songs, which that mixed crowd of people coming from all corners of the word seemed to be so good at. But not a word about the journey or a question asked.

This secrecy made Damanais feel excluded, as he had had for a short time when Ovidius preferred to write his verses with his own hand. Yet he had no choice but to accept his master's decision. Much later, he will understand that, by having hidden certain things, Ovidius was actually protecting him. The same for Dionisodor.

When back in Histria, the merchant gave them a warm welcome, content that he had put the screw on Nicanor to finish the work before the time limit laid down. Dionisodor had not accepted the defeat. Even if he had not succeeded to get a lower price which Ovidius paid anyway, not him, at least he obtained the same quality, for the same money, but in a shorter time.

'Thank you, my friend, for all your help,' the poet worded his gratitude after hearing the good news. 'I am now leaving to Tomis. I have already been absent for some time and, even though no one is breathing down my neck, I would not want to arouse suspicion... The inscription, sealed as is, needs to reach Tertius Valens. He will know what to do with it. But it is crucial the transport be made with the utmost discretion.'

'Consider it done already, my good Naso.'

Chapter 9
Seven hundred seventy
– The alternative

He felt that the spider web woven around him by Aelius Firmus, with spies, had truly unravelled, but it was still there. It had not been difficult to convince Diokles to turn a blind eye to his moves. He had simply told him that he had a text he wanted engraved on his tombstone, but the words themselves, due to the agitation that could have caused, would remain hidden, along with his tomb, forever. What the officer heard was that Ovidius needed some quiet time, space and freedom of movement to carry out his plan and gave his consent. It was Artemon he had to persuade to bring him to an understanding. The archon wanted some evidence, assurance that there would be no loss of information to imperil his position and life, he wanted money, a whole hell of a lot. But finally, he surrendered.

In fact, the entire warp of Ovidius had a very simple message – 'Let me say what I have to say, since my conscience will not let me be quiet and you will not suffer anyway because of my confession, as long as it is post-mortem and I will make sure to rake the ground behind me, as if nothing had happened.' The secret of the tomb became, in this context, part of the arrangement. That there was an inscription in the story, which never dies, that was the gauntlet thrown down at the history.

And there was something else… His entire life, the poet

had made a go of everything. He had done all right for himself, climbed from the bottom to the pinnacle of power, had fallen from up high and broken his wings. He was aware that his name and works would outlive him. In these conditions, he wanted to die quietly, since death is an intimate experience itself and did not want to flaunt the moment of passing. On the contrary. A veil of mystery thrown upon his death could only cement the legend.

It is then he started travelling and his journeys seemed to be controlled by a zeal bordering despair rather than a specific purpose. As if he had felt his end coming closer and wanted to reclaim something... At least that was the impression left at the beginning. Then, while the rumours had spread he had started a new piece of writing (!) to turn into a treatise about fish and fishing, given that he needed to gather information on the land, most agreed that this must have been his intent.

They suspected he had arranged his freedom of traveling between the river and Pontus, even farther, so the gossip stopped.

On the other hand, Aelius Firmus, along with the archon and the officer assumed that under the claimed hunt for resources needed in his work was hiding the search for a secluded spot to camouflage his tomb and gave him a free hand...

One day, he was in Callatis, even though he did not like the city, but he was mingling with the fishermen throwing their nets, south of the city. Another day, he was walking on the isthmus leading to Mesembria.[161] In Histria everyone knew him and some said to have seen him embarking right there, bound for Olbya.[162] People had also seen him in the delta but he had ventured, as some said, as far as the right

---

161   Greek colony, the current city of Nessebar (Bulgaria).
162   Olbya Pontica, Greek colony, at the mouth of Bug river (Ukraine).

shore of Danubius, in the Dacian territory, at Netindava,[163] where barbarians maintained that the divine twins, Apollo and Artemis, had been born.

Damanais was going everywhere with him. He was writing down about the fishermen's life, their trade, fresh water fish and sea fish. He was scrawling legends, lies and charms meant to fill up the nets, yet he was paying attention to his master's words, who kept infusing his mind that when he is no more, the young man should take him out the Tomis gate and carry him on the road to Helios – from Sunrise to Sunset, then to trust his life in the hands of Tertius Valens and his comrades. They will know what to do. He was to be the only Tomitan to know the site of his tomb and he was leaving a legacy in the duty to ensure, on his part, that he would find someone trustworthy to pass on the secret on, along with the duty to guard it and so on, till the end of the world.

'The mystery, my child, will not be the tomb itself, but the stone inscription, which can do a lot of harm. I don't know how the world will be in hundred or thousand years, but I don't want to hurt my country, even though my conscience will not let me keep the things I know in dark. This is why it will not be me speaking, as my lips are sealed forever, but my tombstone will. You just have to ensure that no one hears it. You are wondering, probably, what's the good to bestow a gravestone with the ability to speak and you still want to hush it… Well, this is the price deemed right to pay for my freedom. But, behold! It is my Trojan horse, which I leave at the history gates, just like the Achaeans before the gates of Ilion!'

Unusual and herculean burden for the son of farmer Zourdanos…

---

163   Dacian dava mentioned by Ptolemy, which some researchers identify with the current village Sărăţeni, Vaslui county. The issue is still under debate.

The end of summer found them in Histria, guests in Dionisodor's house. One day before leaving for the delta, in what would have been the last stop in the Scythian journey where they had collected enough material for an entire winter to write their treaty, the merchant had a big celebration to honour his Tomitan friend. The guests came, ate and drank, and left, but Dionisodor seemed to have a heavy heart. The next morning, while seeing off Ovidius and his young disciple, tears were welling from his eyes.

Despite the Dionysian ebullience having taken hold of his house the night before, that seemed to have a mortuary odour, of an imminent farewell, something hidden that Dionisodor knew or sensed.

Did he know or sense it?

Naso was biting his lips. He was also trying hard not to burst into tears. Did he know or sense it? Was it part of his plan, or of the Great Plan?

They hugged. Most of the time, they found something to say, a pledge to see each other soon, a good word to keep company on the road, something... But then... just silence. Both were afraid their voice would be quivering...

Instead, Tertius Valens welcomed them gladly.

'You kept your word, Naso! You came exactly when you said you would! For my part, I will keep my promise and take you with us tomorrow morning, to catch the big fish! Until then, let us be merry!'

... And they were, as if all were Dacians and one of them had passed away.

When the gentle autumn sun woke Damanais up, his master was missing. The few left behind told him that Ovidius, Valens and other seven had left before dawn, by three punts, to the place where the river meets the sea. This is where the gigantic belugas are to be found.

He was only left with counting the hours. And he counted...

And counted… And when he was just about to go out of mind, they came back, yet the poet was not among them. He felt a lump in his throat, all the more that the glances of the others did not look good. And they had nothing good to say! They were coming, wet to the bone, bleary eyes and fists clenched in spite.

Tertius Valens plodded towards him, while his comrades scattered every which way, as if they did not witness to what was about to happen.

The young Get stood up slowly from his seat, looking at the deserter dawdling on his way, like a dark angel.

'My child, come here!' Valens demanded him.

He took two faltering steps, trying to catch the man's eye, but he was looking away.

'Publius Ovidius Naso is dead.'

The words hit him like a hammer on the back of his head. He felt his knees sinking under him and dropped on a rock, his chin trembling.

'His boat was hit by a sea monster. There was nothing we could do. The waves were high… You have to summon up your strength and ride all in a breath to Tomis, to make the arrangements!'

What??? Was that all? This is how trusting his life in the hands of Valens people was, as Ovidius had advised him? Were they banishing him? The poet was dead because of their neglect and they were banishing him? He would have liked to fight back, but he was not able to. The anguish in his heart and the fear that, had he retaliated the way he rightfully felt like, he might have put his life in danger, had numbed his tongue. He sprinted, swung himself into the saddle and off he went!

After a while, late into night, to a briskly dawn, when the horizon is turning on the other side while asleep, with the cheek to what would have been light, yet murky like an aged cheese then, the guards on Tomis ramparts heard a horse clopping, approaching the gates.

The rider tired out the animal so much that the poor horse was half dead when they arrived. Indeed, it made a long neigh and collapsed by the walls. They recognized Damanais and said no words. They let him in, so much more that his gloomy face, where tears had mixed with dust, together with the fact that he had come all in one breath, alone, with no sign of Ovidius, were all pointing to a tragedy.

The boy bolted on the city streets and he only stopped in front of Diokles' house, pounding with his fists and feet upon the gate.

After the vain attempt of the sun to rise, which did not dispel the fog one bit, but only blended things and shadows into an amorphous paste, like the one before Creation, when the boy had simmered down in the overseer's home, Artemon and Aelius Firmus were listening to the story of the anguished disciple.

And darkness was still his witness when Damanais left Tomis alone, in a wagon carrying an empty stone casket bearing Naso effigy.

From up there, on one of the towers, the tribune and the officer were trying to watch him through the fog.

'A simple chronicle, as we talked about,' said Diokles, just for the sake of it.

'Yes,' agreed Firmus, absorbed in his thoughts.

'And the boy?'

'What about him?'

'He is the only one to know where the grave is…'

'Very well. It saves us a lot of trouble.'

'What if he is coming back?'

'He will not. He is not stupid. He will read the inscription and will realize it is best for him not to ever set foot in Tomis. If he does it, though, that is going to be the last mistake in his short life.'

'You are right. Whoever knows that text, becomes a victim.'

'Yes… Just like us…'

And, after a break, the tribune went on…

'Where do you think the grave is?'

'Hm! Right there, beyond the fog,' Diokles answered, pointing to… nothing.

The name of 'Tomis' had already been wiped off from Damanais mind when he left the city. The road was going westwards and he followed it, with no detour, as Ovidius once told him. The Sun Way took him… he had no idea where. He was going into the right direction, but he could not see the end. In fact, he could not even see the sun, but only a blurry source of light, due to the fog. And when you think he should have been the one to know the secret place! But the anguish inside him had swelled and swallowed him entirely, and left no room within or around him for other thoughts. In fact, he did not even make a gesture when Valens people took the reins to stop the horses and the wagon, after they had yelled at him in vain. They were there! They knew it! They had chosen the secret place, together with the poet, some time ago.

*

He saw them, or better to say he was vaguely discerning their shape, but he could not hear them. A terrible rumble in his ears, going all the way into his brain, was numbing him. He could not actually hear the rumble. He was rather living its occurrence, in a way surpassing his feelings. His glance was bouncing off the shades roaming around or did not even reach them. He got a slap in his face from… Gnur (?), but who cared anymore? He was present there only physically. Another one, probably Asphartes, shook him vigorously. Nothing! The shake would have awaken up even Thanatos! It did nothing to him.

At one point, he recognized Valens's face in that milky fog veiling his eyes coming very close to where his face probably was. The deserter's lips moved as if he was saying something clearly, almost barking. Over and over again. He realized he had to read his lips if he wanted to understand something, as he could not hear him: Da-ma-na-is! Da-ma-na-is! He knew the name, but not where he had heard it. Slowly, he started hearing the sounds going along with the moves of those lips.

A new shake.

'Damanais!'

His eyelashes fluttered several times. The face with the lips moved away. Valens ordered to his people.

'Stand aside, he needs air! He came back.'

He was lying on the ground, by the wagon. They helped him on his feet and one of them gave him a goatskin bottle with water. He gulped it.

Valens put his arm around his shoulders.

'Here is the grave, my child. This mound. It is well protected, on this side of the fog.'

He looked around, intently. An obscure ridge was disappearing in the background, with the shrubs of thistles scorched by the sun over the summer. Valens pushed him gently, as an invite, to the *dromos*[164] going down under a short vault, lined up with burnt bricks, into the mound. The room where Ovidius would have slept the sleep that knows no waking, dimly lit by a torch almost gone, had the stone crypt in its middle, simple, with no architectural element to

---

164 Access road to the vaulted Greek and Hellenistic tombs and to the Geto-Dacian tombstones.

disclose the identity of its guest. Nevertheless, above it, the slab was screaming to high heaven.

'Read!' Valens urged him, and the boy leaned over the inscription engrave in stone by Nicanor.

A long sigh gave the Roman to understand that the Get had finished reading. He gestured to look at him, in that light about to go out.

'This is Ovidius' last will,' said Tertius Valens. 'And you must guard it. You and the ones you will choose after you, till the end of the world.'

They walked out. Several of the companions of the former *tesserarius* took the empty urn inside and started sealing the entrance.

'What about you?' he dared to ask.

The deserter smiled, ruffled his hair, almost like a parent, and answered, looking away, at the horizon, as if looking for a certain cardinal point, not knowing which one.

'We are going to be around, nearby. In sight, do not worry. We and our descendants.'

Hard to tell whether that man in Valens's retinue, dressed in a black cloth from head to toes, from under his eyes only were visible and who had kept himself out of the way all the time, was Naso himself, or if he was waiting for the deported home, in their small village beyond the channels, to tell him how his young disciple had received the daunting task to have been given to him.

Chapter 10

Seven hundred seventy
– The last mission

I would be a hypocrite, my reader, if I complained about the time spent in Sulmo, or the contract with the man in the tricolour toga. The small town I had taken up my residence was as pleasant as it could be, so was the host, and the tasks I received during those seven years were about that thing I knew best – to kill. Once only did I ask my master why I had to take a certain life and, as you will see, it was my last mission. Not with the rest. Why? It's simple. The moment you accept to be a chisel, then your task is to let yourself be hit in the head by the hammer and, together, to sculpt a random object. Your task is not to debate on the artist's vision. As a chisel, it is possible to go blunt... This is something else... As a hired assassin, it is possible you regret one or two dead by your hand. This is why it is better you don't know them at all, so you will not risk being fond of them. Should my bizarre master thought necessary to inform me about the reasons, he would do that. If he thought it proper to have me infiltrate in the victim's entourage, then he would set about it.

After Turdus Merula, I drew my breath. It is true, the fact I was forbidden to set foot in Rome was eating my heart out, as I was dying to see Servillia and could not. But it wasn't long before the man in the black-white-red toga sent me to put to death a moneylender. Quick, no complications.

I took my money, did what I had to do and then stopped by Mama Gaia's brothel.

After a while, I went to Capua, to take out a merchant who had the higher-ups of the city under his thumb and was pulling ropes to thwart the transport of the rivals' goods coming from the East.

Before that difficult and strange year – the year when Sextus Pompeius[165] and Sextus Appuleius[166] were consuls of Rome, the seven hundred sixty and seventh, since the founding of Rome – I had had a rich, yet not very grandiose murder record – several military commanders, merchants and moneylenders, a corrupted priest in an obscure temple of a deity equally abstruse… The only noble sent by me to the world of shadows had been Lucius Aemilius Paullus,[167] exposed as part of a conspiracy against the emperor. Such attempts were the talk of the town. I think poor Augustus had already got weary of reacting when he found out something like that. These things happened naturally – the right people intervened and traitors disappeared, one way or another.

Paullus tried to hide, but there was always a shadow on his trail. He even tried to change his name. The shadow knew who he was… He tried to flee Rome. In vain! In the end he only managed to die tired. When he realized the shadow had a face, that he was actually face to face with his executioner and there was nowhere else to hide, he begged for his life. I explained to him I could not do that. He tried to corrupt me with money, which insulted me. Nevertheless,

---

165 Roman general and politician, 1st century BC–AD 1st century , military commander of Moesia during Ovidius trip to his exile place, then consul of Rome in the year AD 14.
166 Roman politician, 1st century BC–AD 1st century, about whose career is only known to have been a consul in the year AD 14.
167 Roman politician (37 BC–cca AD 8–14 AD, consul in the year AD 1.

I fulfilled his last wish – to be killed from behind, for people to find out that the emperor eliminates foully his enemies blah... blah... blah. Oh, well... Coming from a conspirator, it sounded kind of... I for one found it amusing. Yet, as a professional, I only laughed after the killing. I have to admit, Paullus had me running about quite a bit until I caught him...

But the year I wanted to talk about, my dear reader, all of these people seemed to have gone crazy.

'The emperor's health is crumbling,' the man in the tricolour toga told me one day.

I had literally opened my eyes upon him early morning, as was his custom. He had been waiting quietly, leaning on one of the walls, for me to wake up. His coming from nowhere no longer impressed me.

'Good morning to you, too!' I answered, in a sleepy voice.

He made that sound I always took as a laugh.

'It is clear for everyone Augustus will die soon,' he told me after half an hour, while we were taking a nice walk on the streets in Sulmo.

'How so? I thought he was immortal...'

'He is indeed, my friend! The crossing over does not preclude immortality. If we want to discuss the matter and the method, we can do it, but it's not the case this time. What is important now is the succession. Prima facie, it seems that Livia Drusillas efforts bore fruit and that, even if he dislikes it, Augustus consented to Tiberius being the next emperor. As you know, his close grandson, Agrippa Postumus, is exiled on Planasia Island. But Augustus visited him not long ago. Despite the secrecy, the word got out. How? Well, the emperor's good friend, Paullus Fabius Maximus[168]is to blame. He accompanied the emperor and then he confided

---

168　Roman politician, consul in year 11 BC, confident of emperor Octavian Augustus.

to his wife, Marcia, in bed, and she told Livia Drusilla the next day, while babbling to each other. Maximus killed himself, which was as noble as useless of him. The idea is that Augustus, now in Nola, where he is living his last hours among mortals, made things worse by naming Agrippa as his successor and hatching, with him and Maximus, a plan by which the young man should come to take over his duties as *imperator*, once his grandfather passes away. Here, my friend Corvus, we are talking about the volatile state of history, which I once told you about. The steam coming out of the furnace has to be steadfast, otherwise the alchemical work is not complete. If the austral wind blows and the steam is going sideways, this is where the volatile collapses.

'To have Agrippa coming to Rome, that would mean a fatal wind blow – a new civil war. I bet Tiberius, as we speak, is making sure nothing like that happens.

'However, someone, I mean me, has to remind Tiberius and his hired blade, that they are not the salt of the earth and that there is some else on this earth and a few more worlds around it, that is me, who rolls the dice. It is not vanity, but a rightful desire to keep a balance equal to order. Right now, if Tiberius and only he, even through his middlemen, succeeds in eliminating Agrippa, it will give him the false impression he holds the reins of history, hence the possibility of unwanted excess to occur. This is where you come in. You are going to Planasia Island and murder Agrippa. The killers sent by Drussila's son have to find him dead and report this to Tiberius, to give him something to think about.

I got my money, thanked for it and took the road. Hardly had I boarded the ship that was taking me from the port of Naples to the island where target was, that the word about the emperor's death reached my ears. He had died alone, as he had been living, despite the throng gathered around him. I was thinking, with a small smile in the corner of my mouth, how the empress is mourning with one eye, while the other is already riveted to the throne soon to be sat on by her son, Tiberius. Her whole life had been about devising plans and eliminating rivals. There was only one left and she knew that, if she wasn't swift enough, he would come to Rome and blow down the sand castle she had built on blood for some many years. Well... The man in tricolour toga liked to call it 'steam'. I preferred to call history a 'sand castle'...

For a short moment, I pondered that if there was one person my master truly wanted to give something to think about, that was not Tiberius, but Empress Livia Drusilla herself...

The young Agrippa was not even twenty-six. He had inherited from his grandfather, through his mother's blood, eyes of an intelligence that was almost corporal, which you could almost touch; a disarmingly real intelligence. Unfortunately for him, he had also acquired, directly on the maternal side, a free spirit bordering recklessness that, at one point, had exposed him to defamation. In the sumptuous villa where he had been living his exile, he seemed on the go. His grandfather had surely told him he would hear from him and, when that happened, he had to be ready to go to Rome. This is why, when he saw the small sailboat I was on coming close the wharf, he came to welcome me.

His first thought was good, as he smiled and met me with open arms. Then, after seeing I was alone, with no imperial insignia, it dawned on him and his face darkened. He went into the villa and I followed him, closing the door behind us. He sent away the servants and there were only the two of us in the wide hall of his house. He was holding a papyrus roll in his hand. He showed it to me.

'This is my grandfather's declaration, which gives me the right to sit on the throne of Rome, after his death.'

I shrugged.

'I do not dispute that, but this does not concern me. (I took the *gladius* out.) Do not get me wrong. It is neither something personal, nor am I involved in the political games.'

'I understand,' he answered, nodding his head, then he turned his back to me. 'Do it quickly!'

Needless to say, my reader, that, after so much practice, I knew very well that spot between the ribs where the blade goes straight into the heart, so that the man dies fast, without too much pain. I struck the blow and left, not before taking the roll reading indeed Augustus' last wish, which was stripping Tiberius of the privileges publicly granted to him and transferring them to the young man lying at my feet in a pool of blood.

I have told you, my reader that sometimes I felt sorry for the people I had to kill. It happened with Agrippa, despite the rumours that had tarnished his name, at the obvious behest of Livia Drusilla. I had a sense of having held the balance of history in my hands, but the reason for which it had to flow (or to go up, like steam) into a certain direction and not into another escaped me. But it did not my patron, which reminded me of the contract, of Servillia and my rank.

When I sailed away from the shore, my boat crossed paths with a galley on whose board I recognized the dreaded Sejanus.[169] Aha! As everyone knew about the friendship between him and Tiberius, I deduced (correctly, as I found out later) that he was the blade sent to kill Agrippa. I had been faster. The essence of my mission had not been in slaying the young man, but doing it before Sejanus. In conclusion – a real triumph! Whether the *praefectus praetorio*[170]

169   Lucius Aelius Sejanus (20 BC–AD 31), prefect of the Pretorian Guard, confidant of emperor Tiberius.
170   Commander of the Praetorian Guard

and/or Tiberius understood the moral of the story, that I could not predict... It was not my concern either.

I had not been sailing for long when the praetorians set foot on the shore. I burst out into laughter thinking of the long faces they surely made when they saw someone else had been there before them. A few days later, the wheezing of the man in tricolour toga told me that he was also amused. Plus, the fact that I had fetched the Augustan document raised my value in his books... As for what Tiberius, Livia and Sejanus wanted the rabble to believe about Agrippa's death... Hm! Another reason for amusement. The official reports were saying that it was the guards that killed the young pretender to the throne, after manifesting a sudden and unexplained liking for Tiberius. At first sight, the rabble rose to the fly. Later, the yarn with Clemens, Agrippa's slave, who resembled his master like two drops of water and pretended to be him so as to gather an army and claim the throne... The new emperor had a difficult time to subdue him, which did not help his shattered image, well people are always quick to laugh but they forget even more quickly. Besides, the affair with the succession was in the past. The empire had a new ruler, hence there was a continuity and no one could grumble about a real danger in the lack of power, like during the civil wars. Agrippa's assassination, followed by his mother, the exiled Iulia, and her lover, Sempronius Gracchus, remained only stories for the scholars of the future. And for chatter...

I have to admit though, and I can do it now, many years later, that at one point doubt struck me – what if the one I had killed was Clemens, and the 'usurper' was Agrippa? It's not like I had met either of them before... I could not swear to which was which...

Times were tranquil for a while, which meant less work for me. But I could not lament. The man in the tricolour toga was in control of my stipend and life in Sulmo was as pleasant as it could get. I could even say that it is in those days that I chanced upon literature, philosophy, historiography and the idea of this confession came to me. Plato, Xenophon, Aristotle the Stagirite became my friends, and so did the newer writers from around here – Horace, Titus Livius, Catullus, Vergilius.

Living in Sulmo and inevitably passing his villa and having met his wife at one time, it was impossible to wriggle myself out of reading Ovidius's works, even if they were not to my liking... His first and more recent works were circulating somehow on the edge of the law. He had been banned, but he still held the right to correspond, unlike Iulia who had lost it, which surprised me. And he was making full use of this right. His epistles coming from exile were not quite adequate, in spite of a whiny tone, which could have fooled a distracted mind... But, again, it was not my concern to judge these things. I have written some verses myself, but I will spare you, my reader, out of respect... Anyway... Only after the affair with Marcus Scribonius Libo Drusus[171] have I had several tasks, about eliminating some of his disciples. I saw Servillia quite often. I had not told her about my agreement with the toga man. Instead, I was promising her the same time over and over, which was to take her away from there. She would nod her head, but I think she had lost any hope.

In the year seven hundred seventy *Ab Urbe Condita*, when Pomponius Flaccus and Caelius Rufus were consuls, the time for my contract to end had come.

'I have one last mission, but you will have to leave Italy for that,' my patron said.

---

171   Marcus Scribonius Libo Drusus (?–AD 16), an extravagant young man, son of consul Marcus Scribonius Libo, suspected to have plotted against Tiberius. He killed himself.

'You know I am not leaving without my sister.'

'I know. I will let you take her with you.'

'And I am going to do something else, before leaving.'

He wheezed/laughed.

'I can imagine what… I will not object to that. I will see it as an act of civil purging. Until then, let me tell you who I am talking about.'

He told me about the poet Ovidius Publius Naso, his complicity with the court conspiracies, accusations of lèse-majesté, then the exile to the faraway land of Pontus Euxinus, about how he had continued to stir the spirits from there (which I had suspected, by reading his works) and most of all, Tiberius' neurosis. Of course! After a whole life when your mommy has been working on your political career by slaying all your rivals, it is natural to lose your grip and see schemes against him everywhere. Hence the need to liquidate the Sulmonian in Tomis.

'Here is the thing,' I told the man in toga, after he had finished the story. I have never made comments on your decisions and I don't want to think I am going to do it now, so late in the game. Nevertheless, the mission seems senseless. The man has already paid his price. He is probably in his old age and the end is down the street … Why do you need me?'

'Hm… let us go for a walk!'

We took a stroll around the small town of the old *paeligni*[172] and, for a while, we talked about nothing. I already knew his method. He was going to make a confession and, as usual, he was beating about the bush. Suddenly…

'Arrius!' (I flinched, as he had never called me that name and it sounded strangely, almost strangely familiar.) 'Do you remember our discussion about the hemlock?'

I smiled.

---

172   Italic tribe in Valle Paeligna, the current Abruzzo.

'How could I forget? I was the hemlock...'

'Let us see the real plant, not the metaphor... Do you want that? You have heard of Socrates... (I nodded my head.) But do you know the name of his accusers?'

'Not off the top of my head, but I am sure to have read them somewhere.'

'Of course. But what can you tell me about Socrates's death?'

'Oh! The cup of poison? Hemlock?'

'Exactly! You see, hemlock is not a simple poison. Sometimes, it is the path to legend. To have a destiny fulfilled and turn into a legend, you not only need heroes, but also antiheroes. What is Caesar without Brutus? But let us go outside Italy! What would have been Osiris without Seth? Socrates and his cup of poison? Hercules without Nessus' tunic? I could find more examples... The architect in Tyr or... Whatever... Some things happen in a certain way, otherwise people would be left without too many points of reference they can talk about and learn from. As for this last mission of yours, they will be probably talking a great deal about the mystery of death of this Ovidius. The man used to dip his bread with the highest and knows things that are even perilous for him. I have heard he is writing his last will... rather instigative. But this is not the essence herein, but in the fact that this poet will survive his own death through his verses. He is not the only one. He will not be the last. Your mission is not necessarily to kill him, but to cloak his death into an aura of... hemlock, seen as a path into the legend. The mystery... This is what I am talking about! Killing or only letting people surmise that, you will enrich his legacy, perfect his destiny, raise him from among the immortal poets and set him with the Immortals themselves. I see you are looking at me puzzled! No! My duty is not to liquidate one or another, guilty or not. You had to kill people who, probably, in your opinion, were worthy of living. My duty is to make history. Legend is part of history, so creating legends is beyond doubt my mission.'

The following night, along with Servillia, we were gazing at the fire having come from nowhere, swallowing Mama Gaia's brothel. Right above, in the red flame sky, my black bird flew towards Brundisium,[173] where our journey to the land of Gets was about to start. But what mattered most was that Servillia and I were finally together!

Allow me, my reader, to end my confession with the year of seven hundred seventy, even though more years have passed since... I will put an end to it now as I want to leave my past behind, because my black bird has departed from me for good so I have no one to watch me and I can decide my fate on my own and because I want to die in peace, after such a frenetic life. I will stay silent about the rest of the years for the sake of mystery that has to lead Ovidius into legend, because I have come to an old age, because I am now looking at Servillia sweeping in the courtyard helped by our two children and my heart is filling up with that bliss you only feel on the verge of crossing over. Last but not least, I am going to do it from the desire to not defile with empty words the image of this sublime and wild land, the witness of my last and most beautiful years, this *vicus* in the Danubius Delta where people have come from all four corners in the world, former slaves, former soldiers, people who were part of the royalty in their tribes but preferred to flee, former shepherds with no sheep, people who faked their own death... And the two of us.

---

173 Ancient name of the Italian city Brindisi.

Chapter 11
Seven hundred seventy
– The probability

No one should ever bear the silence as much as he has. Nor with the intensity he did. There should be no silence after him. Had gods found any trace of pity in their immortal souls, then they would have banned silence from the land of living and even that of the dead because he, Publius Ovidius Naso had swallowed it all up! Hiding thoughts behind the unspoken should be outlawed!

For a long time, he had been roaming the filthy markets in Tomis, through the sweat and smoky pall, with the buzzing of the fat flies in his ears, only just to catch a rumour that some galley was coming from Italy. And there were plenty. When he saw them from afar, he felt his heart jumping in his chest like an eager Maenad. Very often, he had a papyrus roll with him, ready to be sent home. Any news from there? No. Just silence. After meeting Dionisodor, he did not have to face the miasma of the markets. He found out in time when the boat anchored and how long it was staying in the port. But the silence remained the same.

It is not that he did not receive any epistles. He did. But none of them sent by his friends on the Peninsula mentioned anything about Augustus having relented. That silence brought him to the brink of despair! He should have fathomed long time ago that Augustus cannot be persuaded. The two Iulias, his well-beloved daughter and his granddaughter, both in exile, had not succeeded. Who was he to hold hope? But every time doubt crept in, he kept thinking of Prometheus and Pandora's Box and of Hope that dies last. Tough doubt prevailed anyway, since the moral of the story was not that Hope dies last, but that ultimately it still dies! Still he kept on wandering on the wharfs, getting on board of every ship coming from Italy. Silence!

'From Paullus Fabius Maximus, to Publius Ovidius Naso, greetings! I have received, my beloved friend, your gift. I was glad to see you are alive, but the sight of that quiver with arrows accompanying the book frightened me. It is horrible what is happening to you. You are like my son. Married to a Fabia, you acclaimed our patria more than Vergilius with the Iulias' lineage. I shed tears on your *Fasti*, when you are recounting how the winning Fabia gens fetched the stolen oxen while Romulus was still looking for the thieves and I should be glad when he *"risit, et indoluit Fabios potuisse Remumque / Vincere, Quintilios non potuisse suos."*[174] But I cannot be, my friend, nor can I when you are sending greetings from Pontus and beg for forgiveness that your gift is not worthy of me. *"Nil igitur tota Ponti regione Sinistri / quod mea sedulitas mittere posset erat. / Clausa tamen misi Scythica tibi tela pharetra: / hoste, precor, fiant illa cruenta tuo. / Hos habet haec calamos, hos haec habet ora libellos, / haec uiget in nostris, Maxime, Musa locis! / Quae quamquam misisse pudet, quia parua uidentur, / tu tamen haec, quaeso, consule missa boni!"*[175] No, Ovidius! My gift is

---

174 'He laughed, and grieved that Remus and the Fabii could have conquered when his own Quintilii could not.' Ovidius, *Fasti II*, v.377-378, transl. Demetrio Marin.
175 'So there was nothing in all this region of Pontus, the perverse, that my consideration could send. Still I've sent you Scythian arrows sheathed in a quiver: I pray they might be stained by your enemies' blood. Such are the pens of this shore: such are the books, such is the Muse, Maximus, that flourishes in this place! Though I'm ashamed to

the one undeserving of you, as I am not able to give you the one that really matters.'

Then, Paullus Fabius Maximus killed himself. Period. Beyond that, silence...

Not even the report about Augustus's death brightened his face, as he was still mourning the death of the strongest in the Fabia family. Nor the fact that Octavian's crossing over had happened during the consul term of Sextus Pompeius who had helped him, while governor of Macedonia, make it through to Tomis and even after that. It didn't mean there was still any ray of Hope. It just meant that the man, intelligent and with a survivor instinct, was to pledge loyalty to Tiberius. That's all there was to it!

... And it seemed that all epistles coming from his motherland were fusing into the same simple idea, which everyone was disguising in the most wonderful words. 'Hope is dead! The last or the second to last or... It does not matter! It has died! Accept that, Ovidius!'

'From Sextus Pompeius, to Publius Ovidius Naso, greetings! My dear friend, be glad, as sad as it sounds, that you are not in Rome! The Eternal City is a diseased city. You hear this from someone who begs you, after you have read my epistle, to burn it! If not, we are both in great danger. I beseech you, my friend, in the name of the help I gave you from the bottom of my heart, set my epistle on fire! I wish I could help you again. I read the book you sent me and it hurts to know you are putting so much hope into my consulship, while my hands are tied. You are telling me you had a vision on the Tomis beach and Fame herself said to you, *"En ego laetarum uenio tibi nuntia rerum, / Fama*

---

send them, they seem so poor, still I beg you to take pleasure in their being sent!' Ovidius – *Ex Ponto, III, VIII 'To Fabius Maximus'*, transl. Teodor Naum, in *Ovidius – Scrisori din exil,*, Mondero Publishing House, Bucharest, 2000.

per inmensas aere lapsa uias: / consule Pompeio, quo non tibi carior alter, / candidus et felix proximus annus erit!"[176] Fame is deceitful my friend. I know words travel fast and don't have to tell you that Octavian Augustus joined the immortal gods. I don't know how you feel about it. Actually, I know, but I don't want to commit it to the papyrus roll. I shall have no choice but to dishearten you, my friend, but I am going to…'

He did not even finish reading. He threw the epistle in the fire, as the consul had asked him.

In the meantime, he was getting old. He had written countless epistles. He had sent so much more information than all the finks around, if only for the fact he could not be bought, unlike a fink. He knew what he had sent to Rome and especially to whom! He had taken the heat for the nuisance caused to Augustus every time one of his epistles was reaching Rome and passing from one hand to another, like stolen goods!

The emperor had become unpopular. His rigidness, mostly in his old age, had lost him the admiration of the rabble. They had stopped erecting statues and altars, as it had done after Actium or the campaign in Spain… So, how could he, from the other side of the world, expect to be forgiven by the very man he was trying to rile and was taunting in his writings, against whom he was scheming even from afar by communicating information about the barbarians in the area, the social situation in the Pontus cities, about the ship routes and their affairs? How? It would make more

---

176 'Lo, I, Rumour, come to you with glad tidings, having flown down the vast pathways of the air. Because of Pompei's consulship, he who's dearer to you than any other, the new year will be happy and bright.'
Ex Ponto, IV, IV 'To Sextus Pompeius' transl. Teodor Naum, in *Ovidius – Scrisori din exil* Mondero Publishing House, Bucharest, 2000.

sense to expect a nocturnal visit when an assassin for hire would come and stab him, in the name of the emperor. Or to receive, one day, an epistle asking him to kill himself...

He was fighting a war of nerves. If there was something left to hope for, then that would have been Octavian relenting, not in the sense of forgiving him (the emperor never knew the word 'forgiveness') but rather him saying 'That's enough! I've had enough of that slanderer! The only way to shut his mouth is to summon him back to the country.' He would have shown such benevolence that altars and statues would have started to appear again at crossroads just like after Spain...

Who knows who would have won this war waged from afar? Ovidius or Octavian? Yet death levels all differences, no matter the rank or fortune. The gods wanted Octavian to die first, which was not necessarily a victory for Naso! Anyhow, the story of the two Iulias, one exiled in Pandataria and the other in Tremiti, should have been enough proof of the emperor's stubbornness... Well... It was not even a true stubbornness. The emperor had fallen victim to his own austere laws. So who could have give him any hope? Tiberius? Oh, well... Ovidius hadn't changed his tactics. He tried to rile Tiberius, too, by praising Germanicus. But Tiberius had a lot on his mind... Suffice it to say that the rabble was laughing at him (behind his back) because of how he had barely handled the masquerade of the false Postumus! Ovidius's distant teasing were but child's play... Plus, the new emperor had to negotiate a far more delicate matter – to remove his own mother, whose influence had grown to unhealthy levels. The Senate was revolting. The legions loyal to Augustus were revolting too. And they were countless! Where in the world to have room for the laments of an outcast?

His eyesight was failing him. His fingers were not

following his mind, either. He was dictating to Damanais and very often he would catch himself taking long breaks, as he was lost for words, a sign that his spirit was also declining. Zia was spoon feeding him, even if she was older than him. He would not get out anymore. No reason to do it. Once in a while, the proconsul's emissary was paying him a courtesy visit, if only to check if he was still alive.

'Isn't our good Tiberius Caesar Augustus sending a kind murderer to put an end to my exile?'

Aelius Firmus was smiling. He was surely thinking it was not the case. He was sniffing the air around Ovidius, surmising that the Great and Final Assassin was close, so there was no need for extreme interventions. But what would always come out of his mouth was something completely different.

'My good Naso, what would the world do without your verses? You must live!'

Artemon and Diokles had not crossed his threshold in a long time. He did not miss the old archon. He wished him walking naked and blind through the underworld and have Charon refuse to take him across the river Styx. But Diokles was compassionate. Even if he did not visit, due to his duties, he was sometimes sending him gifts, or some produce, or a slave to help Zia with the cleaning.

The winter of seven hundred seventy *ab Urbe condita* found him ailing. Doctors were shrugging their shoulders. They didn't find it in them to simply tell him it was not a particular affliction, but rather the old age itself! They could not say that in front of the tireless Zia! But Ovidius knew that. He was sensing it. 'Why is there a need, before the great passing, for the man to feel both the ignominy of becoming a burden for the others and the abashment of his own degradation? Why cannot we die while standing?'

And then, again, the question posed to Aelius Firmus.

'Isn't our good Tiberius Caesar Augustus sending a kind murderer to put an end to my exile?'

He had not put any food in his mouth for a few days. He was feeble. Damanais was keeping himself busy around him, as if he was waiting (in vain!) for Ovidius to ask him to sit down to write something. But Ovidius was no longer asking anything. Because Ovidius was dying. He had been fading little by little ever since, at Messalinus Cotta's villa, he received that fateful order from the centurion who had come after him on Ilva Island. He had been waning little by little after he had lost Augustus, his main motivation. He still had just a little more dying to do and that little was being exhausted exactly then, on that winter night...

While he was still in full vigour, he had engraved a kind of last will in stone, through the chisel of a sculptor in Histria, hired by Dionisodor. Tertius Valens had been given the duty (and the money!) to dig a tumulus somewhere, in the middle of nowhere. The tombstone was to wait for Naso there and then to keep him company through the endless ages of time. The young Get was to keep the secret of the last will, and the men of the former *tesserarius* were in turn to keep an eye on his disciple. This double duty was to be passed on as heritage to future generations of watchmen.

When the wagon handled by Damanais got through the Tomis gate, carrying the poet's dead body, there was a fog like the one before Creation. As the clear instructions of the deceased were that only his disciple was to take him to his final resting place, Aelius Firmus and Diokles had to watch him from the ramparts, even if they could barely see anything because of the fog.

'Where do you think the grave is?' Aelius enquired.

'Hm! Right there, beyond the fog,' Diokles answered, pointing to... nothing.

As for Arrius Terentius Corvus, if such a character ever

lived, he then arrived there too late, just to see that the man he had been sent to kill had already received the kiss of death.

'Did you hear that?' the tribune asked from the top of the tower, harking, but Diokles shook his head as a 'No'.

... Yet, his senses had not failed him. It had been indeed a croak like a raven's, yet hoarser, longer and louder.

The end